D0116388

The Road to Chlifa

A NOVEL

MICHÈLE MARINEAU

Translated from the French by
Susan Ouriou

NORTHERN
LIGHTS

Northern Lights Young Novels are published by
Red Deer Press
813 MacKimmie Library Tower
2500 University Drive N.W.
Calgary Alberta Canada T2N 1N4
www.reddeerpress.com

Credits
Cover design by Duncan Campbell
Text Design by Dennis Johnson
Cover photograph courtesy of Ghislain Marie David de Lossy/The
    Image Bank
Printed and bound in Canada by Friesens for Red Deer Press

Acknowledgments
Financial support provided by the Alberta Foundation for the Arts, a
beneficiary of the Lottery Fund of the Government of Alberta, and by
the Canada Council, the Department of Canadian Heritage and the
University of Calgary.

National Library of Canada Cataloguing in Publication Data
Marineau, Michèle, 1955–
[Route de Chlifa. English]
The road to Chlifa
(Northern lights young novels)
Translation of: La route de Chlifa.
ISBN 0-88995-129-2
I. Title. II. Title: Route de Chlifa. English. III. Series.
PS8576.A657R613 1995 jC843'.54 C94-910900-2
PZ7.M37RO 1995

The Road to Chlifa in its original
French edition received the
Governor General's Award, 1993
Alvine Bélisle Award, 1993
Brive/Montreal Award, 1993

BY THE SAME AUTHOR
Cassiopée ou l'été polonais, 1988
(Governor General's Award, 1988)
L'Été des baleines, 1989
L'Homme du Cheshire, 1990

BY THE SAME TRANSLATOR
The Thirteenth Summer
by José Luis Olaizola, 1993

AUTHOR'S NOTE

Both the story and characters in The Road to Chlifa *are fictional. However, the setting for the story is real. This means I had to call on a number of "informers" in order to give an accurate view of certain historical or human aspects. I would like to thank the people without whom this book would not have seen the light of day. First, Pierre Major, as well as the students, teachers and administration of the Émile-Legault Composite High School (in Saint-Laurent), who welcomed me on several occasions and made it possible for me to begin to have a better understanding of the reality that newcomers to Quebec face. Also and especially my young Lebanese friends, Maha and Hiba Kalache, and Maha and Racha Katabi, who were so patient and understanding in answering my numerous questions and in revealing many aspects of their ravaged country. If, despite all my efforts and research, there are any errors or inaccuracies in the text, I would like to state clearly that I am solely responsible for them. Finally, I would like to thank the Canada Council for its financial assistance, which allowed me to finish this project.*

—MICHÈLE MARINEAU

TRANSLATOR'S ACKNOWLEDGMENTS

I would like to thank Dennis Johnson and Tim Wynne-Jones for their unfailing support, Carolyn Dearden, Pat Roy and Vicki Mix for their helping hands, and Maureen Ranson for being my second pair of eyes.

—SUSAN OURIOU

To the children of war

THE MIDDLE EAST

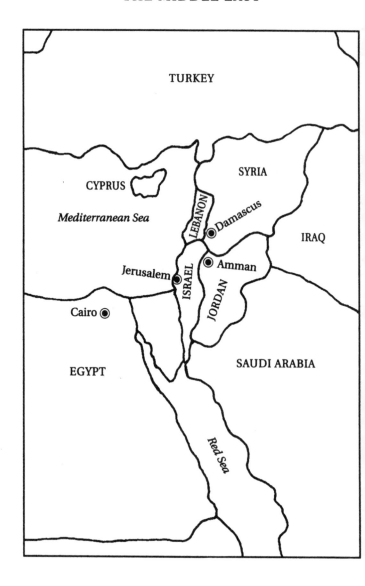

LEBANON

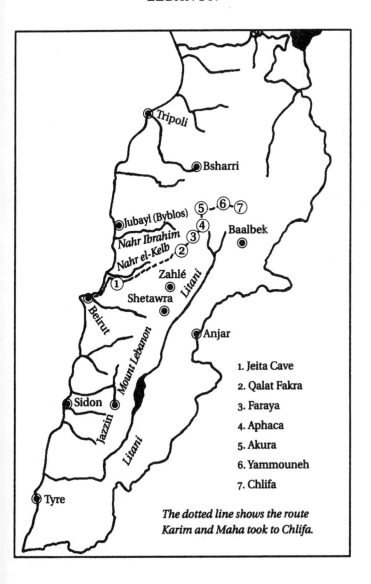

1. Jeita Cave
2. Qalat Fakra
3. Faraya
4. Aphaca
5. Akura
6. Yammouneh
7. Chlifa

The dotted line shows the route Karim and Maha took to Chlifa.

PART I

Catalysis

Montreal, January – February 1990

CATALYSIS: the change in a chemical reaction brought about by a substance (catalyst) that is unchanged chemically at the end of the reaction. *–Webster's*

It was on January 8 that Karim burst in on our lives. On January 8 that it all started.

Actually, no one had noticed the new kid before Nancy walked into class and exclaimed with her usual discretion, "Wow! Is that our Christmas present?"

All eyes focused on "that," a guy sitting in the last row almost at the back of the classroom. Then, in an unusual silence and in front of twenty-eight pairs of particularly attentive eyes, Nancy launched her attack on the newcomer.

"What's your name?"

"Karim."

"That's Arab, isn't it?"

"Yes."

"You an Arab?"

"Yes."

"Where you from?"

"Lebanon."

"Not much of a talker, eh?"

Nancy waited for an answer that didn't come. Then, just as she was getting ready to ask another question, Robert's voice rang out. Robert, the French teacher, had just walked in without anyone noticing.

"Obviously, not everyone is as much of a talker as Nancy Chartrand. Right, Nancy?"

Nancy shrugged her shoulders, unconcerned. "You're the one who's always saying to be nice to new kids, include them in the group and all that. You should be happy I'm so welcoming."

"Happy maybe, surprised definitely. It seems to me you're not always so quick to welcome newcomers."

"Maybe not, but *this one*, at least, is cute. . . ."

All the girls noisily agreed. The boys just looked disgusted. "A bloody Arab," muttered Dave. "If that's what it takes to turn her on . . . "

"Okay," continued Robert, "now that we know Nancy's taste in men, maybe we can start our class. But first, I'd like to welcome Karim. Karim Nakad, is that right?" he added, consulting a small piece of yellow paper.

"Yes, Sir," replied Karim as he stood up, earning a contemptuous laugh from Dave and his gang.

"A word of advice," said Robert. "Stay seated when you answer and call me Robert. That will keep certain people from cackling like a clutch of dizzy hens. Okay?"

The new kid merely nodded before sitting down again. Nancy was right. He really wasn't much of a talker.

"Perfect. Now let's go back over the past participle rule for reflexive verbs, which you had so much trouble understanding before Christmas and which I'm sure you studied every day over the holidays. Reggie, tell me, what do you remember about . . . "

While Reggie tried his best to come up with the wretched rule, the rest of the class, except for a few keeners, turned to the usual pastimes—open-mouthed gawking, the occasional yawn, nose picking, nail filing or people-watching. I must say that people-watching was at an all-time high that day. Or rather, the watching of one particular person—Karim, the new kid.

Nancy was right about his looks, too. This guy was cute. So cute he seemed kind of out of place in the classroom. I mean, he would have looked more at ease against a backdrop of sand and sky, straddling a superbly disdainful camel or a proud steed galloping through the dunes. Now don't ask me if there are deserts or camels in Lebanon. I don't have a clue. But it gives you an idea of his look—the desert prince type, wild and fierce. Tall, slim, delicate features, dark skin, black tousled hair, piercing gaze. The exact image of the fearless hero beyond reproach, the kind you'd love to see fly to your rescue in a fire, an earthquake . . . or a chemistry exam.

KARIM'S DIARY
JANUARY 10, 1990

The hardest part, my little brothers warned me, is the indifference, the impression that you're invisible. And when you finally feel like you do exist, it's because you're in the way or you've messed up somehow. . . .

Well, little brothers, if only that were true! That's all I wanted—isolation, indifference and invisibility—on my first day in this hellhole called a high school. So much for indifference! It felt more like I was a carnival freak or some animal being inspected by potential buyers. That one girl, Nancy, I'm surprised she didn't pry my mouth open to have a look at my teeth!

And all the teacher does is make jokes and try to be pals. If he thinks I need his sympathy or his friendship, he's kidding himself. I don't want anything from him or from the others.

I hate this school. I hate this city.

I hate this life.

When I try to understand everything that happened, I tell myself that Karim had the effect of a catalyst. Like in chemistry class when just adding one substance sets off all kinds of reactions.

Before Karim came, a certain balance had been struck in the class. I wouldn't go so far as to call it a love-in or perfect harmony. Let's just say it was livable. In other words, in spite of different tastes, attitudes, personalities and cultures, we managed to live side by side without killing each other. Not bad considering the violence flaring up everywhere all the time, to the media's delight.

And then, overnight, everything was thrown out of whack because a guy who wanted nothing to do with anyone had a knack for stirring up passions. As though his just being there had stripped away all the politeness, all the compromises, all the habits we used as buffers to let us be in the same place without bumping into one another. We finally showed who we really were, our hatreds, our wants, our prejudices, our dislikes, our petty fears. . . .

Everybody wanted to get hold of Karim, use him for their own ends.

In most cases, it was easy to see how everyone felt and what they wanted and how they tried to get it, too. Almost all the girls were captivated by Karim and wanted nothing more than to melt away the reserve he showed to one and all. And all the guys, or almost all—especially Dave and his gang—resented the way Karim monopolized the girls' dreams and desires.

Among the love-struck there was, of course, Nancy, who, since she'd noticed Karim first, thought she had a hold over him. Her approach, which wasn't too subtle, at least had the advantage of being clear. Right on the first day, she sidled over to him and, while sliding her hand along his thigh, murmured, "Is is true that Arabs are hot-blooded?" Her voice dripped with innuendo. That day, even though she never found out whether or not Arabs are hot-blooded, we all saw that they sure could have an icy stare. Not that it cooled Nancy's passion. Last we heard, she still hadn't given up hope of seducing him.

But not everyone used the same methods. Maybe everybody wanted something different from the new kid.

For example, Sandrine would have liked to recruit him for her—just wait till you hear this—"Consciousness-Raising Committee on the Situation of Immigrants." No less!

Okay, I might as well say it right off the bat—I don't like Sandrine. Maybe because she always wants to run the show. Maybe because she thinks she's the savior of the world in general and of "poor immigrants" in particular. Maybe just because she's doing something when all I do is sit back, watch and take notes. The fact is, she gets on my nerves. And she got on my nerves even more than usual the way she hovered around Karim. But I knew what she was up to. She wasn't having much luck with her committee and had managed to rope in only the most forlorn of the newcomers. A few Asians, a South American, a Haitian—all girls. She must have thought her protégées didn't quite cut it. She wanted a more imposing, more energetic model . . . more virile, above all. And Karim fit the bill perfectly. But she came up against a cold wall of silence, too. And when she turned away, with My-Lan and Maria Gabriella tagging behind as usual, everyone knew she wouldn't give up that easily, that she would launch one attack after another as long as Karim wasn't in her net.

In short, everyone kept watching the new kid, following his every move, hounding him. Some to try to seduce him, others to make him shed his indifference, still others to make fun of what they called his "stuck-up air" and the way he spoke "French from France."

"So you went to the French lycée in Beirut," Dave enjoyed repeating after we found out this fact. "I gotta say, for an Arab, you really think yer hot shit. . . . Hey, you aren't queer, are you? That why you don't want nothing to do with dreamboat Nancy?"

But even these insinuations, accompanied by coarse laughter and vulgar gestures, couldn't get a rise out of Karim.

No one left him in peace. Not even me, now that I'd finally found a good subject to observe and analyze. Later, I'm going to be a writer.

KARIM'S DIARY
JANUARY 16, 1990

It's cold out. I hate the cold and the snow.

The streets here are endless, lined with strange, unfriendly houses. There are no bombs, but then there's no sun either. Or only a cold, insensitive one.

What am I doing in this country?

JANUARY 22, 1990

Got a letter from Béchir, a refugee with his family in Paris now. It hit me how homesick I am for the gang from the lycée, for my friends, especially for Béchir, my lifelong friend. Why does he have to be so far away? To him, at least, I think I could tell the whole story. But he'd have to be across from me with his big grin and his ears that stick out. I can't tell him in writing. In the letter I sent him, all I did was describe my life here as maliciously as I could. I laid it all on him. The cold, the grayness, the ugliness, the accent that grates on my ears, people's stupidity, the lack of respect, the laxness, the vanity and the shallowness, the promiscuity. . . .

JANUARY 27, 1990

Dreamt about M . . . running through the snow. When she turned to me laughing, it wasn't M . . . anymore but a girl from French class, Vietnamese or Chinese or Cambodian, something like that, who looked up at me with her little hypocrite's eyes and her ever-apologetic smile. How dare that China girl steal my dream? What right does she have to . . . Oh! How can I stop this pain?

FEBRUARY 3, 1990

Even from such a distance—although he's never been known for his intuition or subtlety—Béchir knew things weren't going well. In my letter, he picked out forty-two things I hate or detest. He suggested that I 1) vary my vocabulary a bit (I abhor, I loathe, I execrate, I revile . . .), and 2) draw up a list of at least twenty-one things I like here. And to inspire me, he gives me a list of twenty-one things he likes in Paris. They range from the name of a street (Rue du Pot-de-Fer), to the taste of croissants, through the great principles of Peace, Liberty, Equality, Fraternity . . . and a Parisian girl named Lolote (now there I think he's gone too far).

Béchir, old friend, for your sake I'll try, but if I lived here a hundred years, I'm sure I'd never find twenty-one things to like in this god-awful country.

He also asked me, very tactfully, whether I'd heard about the death of the Tabbara family. Well, yes, old pal, I heard, I heard. Do you want the lowdown? The juicy details? SHIT!

FEBRUARY 6, 1990

Haven't answered Béchir yet. I'm still looking for the first of the twenty-one things. On the other hand, the list of things I hold in contempt (how about that for varying my vocabulary?) is growing before my eyes.

For the time being, most of them have to do with school. Everything is pathetic in that dump. The lighting, the "decor," the grub, the blaring of the student radio. And especially the people—teachers and students combined.

As for what we're learning, now that's a real joke. Right now in French, for instance, we get to give oral presentations. In other words, someone picks a song—the more insipid the better, going by what I've heard so far— has the others listen to it, then, for several excruciating minutes, gives his or her "feelings" on the song: "Like, well, I think that . . . really, it means, like, love is fun, but sometimes it's a drag. That's kinda what I think it means. And I think it's right on." Fascinating stuff.

I got out of that chore by telling Robert, the teacher, that I never listen to music and that we don't have a radio or a tape recorder or anything of the kind at home. "It's against our religion," I claimed. I don't know if he believed me, but he didn't insist. The whole time I was dishing it out, I couldn't stop snickering inside. Gone the perfect young man who refused to lie. Gone forever. But there's no one left anymore to care.

FEBRUARY 7, 1990

Two blows today. Twice, words like fists got past the times tables I recite to myself to kill time and forget the idiots stumbling through their presentations up front. Words like fists that hit me full in the stomach and hurt enough to make me scream.

. . . in the boughs of the juniper tree . . .

I didn't dream it. I really did hear "in the boughs of the juniper tree." That Chinese girl was up front, with her little smile and her little eyes, talking about the boughs of the juniper tree. What does that idiot know about juniper trees? What does she know about juniper branches and the wind wailing through juniper branches and the red earth split by juniper roots?

I held back. I didn't throw myself at her, force her to shut up. In silence, I took the hammering of words so excruciatingly gentle:

Cry, birds of February
For the dire chill that fate disposes
Cry, birds of February
Cry for my tears, cry for my roses
In the boughs of the juniper tree

Then afterward came that other girl, the one who's always watching me but who never says a word.

As it was, she said nothing at all before turning the tape recorder on.

A woman's voice rang out:

Man can take nothing for granted.
Not his strength, his weakness, his heart. . . .

I'd never heard the song before, but right away I knew I didn't want to hear it. I didn't want to know what was coming. It could only be terrible.

I was right.

My one love, my true love,
my laceration
I carry you inside like a wounded bird

"NO!"

I cried out. I was on my feet. I felt all eyes on me, but I cared nothing for their eyes and their questions. I could still taste the burning in the back of my throat. The tape recorder kept playing, and the words fell one after another, inexorably, like drops of blood.

I grabbed my books and managed to leave the classroom without falling.

Some images are unbearable.

FEBRUARY 8, 1990

When all's said and done, I prefer insipid songs and morons for whom life is reduced to the slogan some of them wear on their T-shirts: "Don't worry. Be happy." After all, what are wars, death, bombs, orphans, fear, remorse and tears? Real tragedy is not having enough styling gel or lipstick, or forgetting to turn on the VCR to tape the hockey game or the Thursday night soap.

Or, in my case, it's having to go on a three-day "class ski outing" with all these morons. We leave tomorrow. What a prospect.

After a few weeks, we could have gotten bored with the mystery and the resistance, too. But no, we wouldn't give up. We nurtured the mystery, tried to break down the barrier of resistance.

Since we didn't know much about Karim, we made things up according to what we saw or thought we could guess.

One Monday morning, for instance, a crazy, unverifiable rumor started and spread like wildfire. "Did you know Karim has a baby?"

A girl from his math class had met him in the park on Sunday afternoon with a baby.

"Is that your little brother?"

"No."

"Your cousin, then?

"No."

"Someone you're baby-sitting?"

"No."

This rather terse exchange gave rise to the wildest theories. Karim had a mistress, a married woman who had to get rid of her baby at birth. Karim had been married at fifteen to a twelve-year-old who died in childbirth (who knows what customs those countries have?). Karim had had a torrid, illicit love affair ended by the birth of the child and the disappearance of the young girl. . . .

Did Karim himself hear all these stories? I don't know. But they served to keep the curiosity about him alive.

Then there was the episode in French class that I unknowingly triggered—and still don't understand.

My-Lan had just finished giving her presentation on the song that begins "Ah! How the snow falls free. . . ." from a poem by Émile Nelligan, and I was starting my presentation. I'd decided to discuss the song "No Love Without Sorrow" sung by the French singer Barbara. It's based on a poem by Aragon with music by Georges Brassens. I don't know if there's any truth to the title, but I like the song, the way it's dignified and tragic at the same time.

I turned the tape recorder on. Since I wasn't too comfortable standing alone in front of the class, I was looking down at the tips of my shoes, wondering why I'd worn those socks when all of a sudden someone screamed. Glancing up, I saw Karim, on his feet, looking totally shattered. There was nothing left of cold indifference in him. In his eyes were rage, horror, fear, but mostly a terrible sadness. That's when I understood the newcomer wasn't haughty or disdainful like some said. He was simply in despair.

SO KARIM CONTINUED TO INTRIGUE US. And the Karim effect, the Karim catalyst effect, raged on.

Tension, clashes, run-ins had never been as frequent as during the weeks following his arrival. Not a day went by without a fight breaking out in the cafeteria or by the lockers. Not a week went by without students getting suspended from school for a couple of days at a time. In class, the insults and blows flew hard and fast. Dave's gang was particularly bad. They attacked Karim, of course, but also anyone else they didn't like the look of.

"Hey, Reggie the fairy, no, Régine the queen, you getting any lately? That why you're so tight-assed?"

"Hey, fatso. Sandrine. Does it turn you on, listening to all those hard-luck stories?"

"Hey, Nancy, till you catch your Arab, how 'bout letting us cop a feel?"

Simply put, they were acting tough and doing a thoroughly convincing job of it. Probably deep down they weren't really mean, and if someone had based a TV miniseries on them, everyone would have cried buckets over their past, present and future misfortunes. But having to put up with them every day in class didn't make us want to bawl in compassion, only scream in rage. A matter of one's perspective.

Be that as it may, as my grandma would say, it was in this positively explosive atmosphere that we left for our class ski outing. Not surprising that what happened happened.

In fact, it wasn't really a class ski outing but a weekend up north organized by Robert, the French teacher. He organizes one every year, claiming it helps us get to know each other better and promotes team spirit. As for us getting to know each other better, he's probably right. At least, it means you know the color of everyone's pajamas and their brand of toothpaste. As for team spirit . . . let's say that, at first glance, it didn't have the anticipated result.

The good-byes before the bus pulled off were pretty standard, in other words a cross between an earthquake and the end of the world, with cries, tears and gnashing teeth.

The trip was made amid noise and confusion with Sandrine on one side wanting us to sing stuff like "Alouette, Gentille Alouette" and "Frère Jacques," and Dave and his gang on the other side screaming smutty versions of the same songs while taking turns swigging from a bottle of cheap gin.

The driver, stoic or deaf, managed to deliver us safe and sound, which was an achievement in itself.

When we arrived . . . But maybe I don't need to describe every last detail of the weekend or say what we ate for breakfast, lunch and supper, who washed the dishes and who dried, who snores and who doesn't. I'll just describe the events that stood out the most, or at least the ones that, in hindsight, seem charged with meaning.

Like Karim's smile—his first smile!—when he glided all the way to the lake on cross-country skis. Or his look of hatred when My-Lan dropped onto her back in the snow and made an angel with her waving arms. Or his silence, once evening rolled round, when Robert wanted "freshly minted Quebecers to talk about their experiences."

To tell the truth, at first it was mostly Sandrine who "talked about the others' experiences." I've already said I don't like Sandrine. So, inevitably, what she said got on my nerves. I felt like I was in a religion class given by a particularly boring and preachy teacher.

" . . . awful, you know, when you don't understand the language or the customs. When you don't clue in to anything going on around you. When you're faced with situations that go against what you've always believed in, against the principles of your family or your religion. My-Lan, for instance, arrived here three years ago. . . . Couldn't speak a word of French . . . one of her sisters killed in front of her eyes . . . the war . . . their escape . . . the fear . . . shocked by what she sees . . . her twenty-two-year-old sister isn't even allowed to go out alone with a boy, so you can imagine that what goes on in the school halls . . . "

And then, just when I was trying to forget Sandrine's voice—and My-Lan's eyes obstinately fixed on the section of floor in front of her—and concentrate on the flames flickering in the fireplace, on the smell of burning logs and the crackling of the fire, other voices began to pipe up.

"What struck me when I arrived here," said Tung, "was the ethnic diversity. It was the first time I'd seen so many white people, the very first time I'd seen blacks."

"And me," retorted Pascale with a burst of laughter,

"it was the first time I'd seen an Asian. They're not a common sight in Haiti."

One after the other, Ernesto, Ali, Tung, Maria Gabriella, Pascale and My-Lan talked about what had surprised, shocked, touched, intrigued or frightened them. Only Karim stayed silent.

"Snow," sighed Maria Gabriella. "It's so cold."

"Yes, but it's beautiful!" exclaimed My-Lan.

"The girls are beautiful, too," remarked Ernesto.

"Me, I like the ones in my country better," said Ali scornfully, amid protests from the local girls.

They were all struck by how much less important discipline and respect were than in their countries.

"At first," confessed Tung, "I was really shocked by what seemed to me like rudeness, cheekiness, indecency even. I felt like kids didn't respect anyone enough— their parents, their teachers, adults in general, even each other. Now I'm more used to it. I still find some attitudes too aggressive, but there are a lot of things I like. You can speak more freely, give opinions. Sometimes, though, what I learn in school or on the street is hard to fit in with my parents' ideas."

In his corner, Dave and his gang were acting like jerks (nothing much new there). At first, they commented on almost everything being said. "Poor baby!" "You don't say!" "How retarded can you get?" They finally got tired of their game (or else they ran out of dumb and pointless things to say). They started pretending to snore, fart and burp. Then they started trying to paw Nancy, Violaine and Karine, the vamps as I call them—"The jerks and the vamps." It sounds like the title of a fable from La Fontaine—"The jerks of the band/had time on their hands/After playing their games/For most of the day. . . ."

"And racism?" asked Robert at one point. "Do you feel any racism around you?"

Sandrine, who for quite a while had desperately been trying to get back into the conversation, pounced on the subject enthusiastically.

"Ideally," she said in a shrill voice, "one day we'll all look alike, pale brown, and we'll all speak the same language, Esperanto."

Right away, Pascale exploded.

"No way! Your ideal's for robots, for cowards who hate surprises more than anything or having their comfort and little routines disturbed. Everyone alike! What happens when someone's born with green spots or just one arm or two heads? What happens if someone's ideas are kind of different or they have weird tastes?

"Me, for instance, I love my differences. I love my black skin, my laugh that some people find too loud, the way I move that some people find provocative. I don't want to be like everyone else. Believe it or not, not everyone dreams of being white. I've had it up to here with talk about visible minorities, ethnic groups, immigrants. I'm not a visible minority or an ethnic group. I'm Pascale Élysée, born Haitian, a Quebecer by adoption and by choice, living in Quebec and determined to make a life for myself here. I'm black, yeah, but mostly I'm a sixteen-year-old girl who likes chemistry, Marjo, Kevin Costner and BBQ chicken. Everyone always talks about immigrants as a block—"they" this or that—and I can't stand it. We aren't all alike. And when anyone bothers to try to see the differences, they lump us together by country of birth or skin color or religion. Asians are so polite and hardworking, they don't bother anyone, teachers love them. Muslims are bigamists, or polygamists, they don't eat pork, they don't drink, they treat their women like livestock. Hispanics are macho skirt-chasers. Blacks reek, and they're noisy and lazy, etc. It's no more intelligent than saying Quebecers are racists, intolerant bigots. Those big blocks don't exist. What does exist are unique individuals who shouldn't be judged before you get to know them. In my case, I demand the right to be me and not some curiosity or ethnic specimen. I don't want to be called on only as a visible minority to tell my "story" or give the scoop on voodoo, Creole, typical dishes or the best beaches in Haiti. I demand the right to have many characteristics, sometimes even contradictory ones, but that are mine. And I don't intend to spend my life thanking you for having welcomed me to Quebec. I don't intend to keep my eyes down, my voice subdued so as not to draw attention to myself. Whether you like it or not, I'm here to stay and to live, and not just as some exotic, folksy ornament."

Pascale stopped a minute to catch her breath.

I needed a break, too, to digest it all. Really, Robert's idea was a good one. Pascale's tirade opened up new avenues of thought for me. And maybe we might have explored some of them that night if Dave (who else?) hadn't kept being a jerk.

"Hey you, the ornament, shaddup," he yelled from his corner. "You're making such a racket, I can't concentrate on Nancy."

He tickled Nancy who started to squeal. He kept on tickling her, and she began twisting her body every which way. He went a bit further with his tickling, and she stretched right out on top of him.

"Okay, okay, it's getting late. I think it's time for bed," announced Robert.

"Attaboy, Bob, now you're talking!" Dave yelled, pretending to drag Nancy behind him.

"Boys in one dormitory, girls in the other," specified Robert in a particularly firm tone.

"Oh, right. We might shock the little imports. Whadda

you say, My-Lan?" sniggered Dave in her direction. "One of these days though, we're gonna hafta loosen you up a bit. . . ."

And with a crude, totally scornful laugh, he headed to the boys dormitory, his gang on his heels.

I woke up with a start, my heart pounding. Something was happening, I was sure of it. But what?

Around me, others were starting to stir as well.

"What's going on? It's not time to get up yet. It's still dark out. . . ."

"I heard a cry. . . ."

"There was a kind of boom. . . ."

Suddenly, there was no longer any doubt. A wail echoed through the walls.

"Christ! Do something! He's gonna kill him!"

Dull thuds, muffled exclamations, then a new cry.

"NO!"

Only then did we race toward the boys bathroom where all the racket was coming from.

I'll never forget the scene that met us. Every detail was thrown into relief by the stark neon lights.

On the ground, in what could only be called a pool of blood, lay Karim. Standing beside him, looking wild, his lips split, his eye mangled, was Dave, a bloody knife in his hand. At a safe distance, Dave's friends stood in a circle. Finally, in a corner, her housecoat askew, was My-Lan, who seemed paralyzed with terror.

Dave's lips started to tremble, and he raised an incredulous, horrified gaze toward us all huddled together at the door, not daring to step inside.

"He tried to kill me. He's a friggin' maniac. He was gonna kill me. . . ."

And he started to cry with huge, raucous sobs.

"But now you killed him. . . ."

"I dunno. . . . I didn't mean to kill him. . . . I swear I didn't mean to kill him. . . . I just wanted him to let go of me. . . . Just to let go . . . "

We would probably have stayed rooted to the spot until the end of time if, all of a sudden, Simon, usually the quiet type, hadn't murmured, "Maybe he isn't dead," thus triggering feverish operations to check his vital signs (Karim, in fact, was not dead) and go for help (even though he was alive, his condition required immediate care).

Hurried footsteps criss-crossing the building, phone calls, the wait, the ambulance's arrival, transporting the victim to the closest hospital . . .

Only after Karim's evacuation did we find out what had happened. . . . And even then, the witnesses' accounts didn't always agree and were a long way from explaining everything. I'll just stick to a brief chronological sketch of what happened.

Late at night, Dave and his gang camped out in the boys bathroom to empty a bottle of vodka. To each his own.

At one point, they heard a noise in the hall. Glancing out, they caught sight of My-Lan hurrying toward the kitchen.

"Hey, hey," murmured Dave. "The little import. What about us having some fun, boys?"

So they intercepted My-Lan in the hall and asked what she was doing there.

"It's not safe to be wandering around in the dead of night. Lots of things can happen in the dead of night. But maybe that's just what you're after. . . . You off to find your lover?"

"No. I'm going for a glass of water. The spaghetti at supper made me thirsty."

The boys laughed.

"A glass of water. We got somethin' way better to offer you, My-Lan. Way better."

They dragged her with them into the bathroom and, despite her attempts to escape, forced her to swallow a good glassful of vodka.

Then they felt her up a bit.

"Just for fun," they said afterward. "We wouldn'a hurt her, and we wouldn'a raped her. We just wanted to have some fun, teach her a thing or two. That's all."

We'll never know for certain. We'll never know whether, in the heat of the moment, they wouldn't have gone further than they intended.

One thing is certain, My-Lan definitely did not like what was happening. She fought them, tried to escape, to call out.

And then, all of a sudden, Karim appeared from nowhere.

"Let go of her."

"Cool it, Arab. Don't spoil our fun."

"Leave her alone."

"When we're through, we'll let you have her. Promise. Then you can do what you want with her. Even if she is kinda flat, but—"

Dave didn't get to finish his sentence before Karim went for him.

"Christ, he just about killed me. I never seen such a madman."

The others confirmed that Karim kept pounding Dave like crazy, acting like he wouldn't let him go until he knocked him out . . . or killed him.

Luc, Dave's best friend, had a switchblade in his pocket. He slipped it to Dave, who struck out in front of himself, wildly, blinded by the blows that kept raining down on him.

"I just wanted him to let go of me, I swear. I just wanted him to let go."

KARIM'S DIARY
FEBRUARY 14, 1990

I woke up in the hospital. Surprised to still be alive. Disappointed almost.

Three cracked ribs, a split eyebrow, a broken tooth. And this great gash which, apparently, just about did me in. "Three-quarters of an inch farther and it would have been all over, my boy," the doctor said.

It's strange, all the same, to come through fourteen years of war unscathed and then just about buy it in Saint-Donat, Quebec, where bombs and shells must be quite rare, thanks anyway.

Not that it wouldn't have been . . . what? A solution? Yes, maybe a solution. Quick. Final. Soothing. No more dreams. No more memories. No more remorse. Bliss, in other words. On top of which, I'd have died a hero. . . . What a joke, what a monumental joke!

I was dreaming. Always the same dream. The one on the mountain, after the cry, when I'm running, not knowing what to expect. I don't know what woke me, but there I was sitting up in bed, out of breath, my heart beating fast. That's when I heard a door close, a muffled cry. Right away I knew it was coming from the washroom. So that's where I went. I opened the door. Even before I saw them, I knew they were there. I knew she was there. I knew it all along. They were holding her. They were touching her. There was so much fear in her eyes, so much horror, so much . . . Time stood still. Everything else disappeared. They were all that was left. And her. I stepped inside, and I hit out again and again and again and again. . . .

A LITTLE LATER

My-Lan just left. You should have seen her expression when the nurse opened the door with a flourish and said, "There he is, my dear, there's your fella, a little worse for wear." And to me, "You never told me you had such a darling girlfriend. Did you see the beautiful flowers she brought you for Valentine's Day? I'll leave you two alone, but . . . be good now!"

At first, My-Lan kept busy finding a vase for the flowers, then some water for the vase, then a place to set the vase down. . . . Afterward, with nothing left to do, she sat on the edge of the chair next to the bed.

"I can't stay long. I told my parents I was going to Sandrine's house to study. I . . . I wanted to thank you."

I can't stand thank-yous. Especially when they're undeserved.

"Thank-you for what you did for me, especially since I know you don't like me much. So . . . "

She's got it wrong. She's got it all wrong. But how can I tell her?

My-Lan stood up to leave. I still hadn't said a word. I just couldn't let her leave like that, with her pathetic air and her empty hands. So I said, "She's right. The flowers are beautiful." And I added, really fast before I could change my mind, "I'm sorry. I'm tired today. But you can come back tomorrow if you like." She didn't say anything. She bit her lip, bowed her head and left.

What possessed me to ask her back? Do I really want to keep up the false pretense? She thinks I did it for her. But it wasn't for her that I stepped in. It was for M . . . No, not even. For me.

PART II

The Mountain that is Lebanon

Beirut – Chlifa, Lebanon, June 1989

> He who stays is a stone
> He who goes is a bird
> *–Lebanese proverb*

At the first glimmer of dawn, in the brief lull separating the night's shelling from the day's, Karim hurries along Mar Elias Street in the direction of the Mazraa district where Nada lives.

It's his first outing in three days and, despite the still-smoking ruins, despite the danger lurking around every corner, despite the isolated gunshots, some close by, Karim is happy. Finally, he feels that he can breathe again. He's had enough of making the trip between the empty apartment and the cellar, enough of this confined, stagnant existence.

"A real rat's life," he murmurs, looking up at the pale blue sky, so clear.

This rat's life, as Karim calls it, has gone on for three months—since the bombing started again, as fierce as during the worst moments of this seemingly endless war.

The war has lasted for so long that Karim has no recollection of what Lebanon was like *before*. To tell the truth, his earliest memory actually dates back to the first "official" day of war, April 13, 1975.

It was a Sunday, a Sunday of brilliant sunlight, warm breezes, exciting smells. A real holiday for Karim's third birthday. In the afternoon, after his nap, his father had promised to take him to Pigeon grotto on the seashore. After the outing, there would be a ride on the ferris wheel at the beach and a picnic.

But just as they were about to leave, the telephone rang. Hastily excusing himself, his father left without Karim. He stayed away for hours and hours. The outing didn't take place. Karim threw a temper tantrum that his mother still talks about after all this time, one he's a bit ashamed of when he thinks of the greater drama that began on that day.

The reason his father rushed off was to make his way

to the Aïn Remmaneh district where violence had just broken out between Christians and Palestinians. There was talk of provocation, shots fired, a massacre. . . . Karim's father was a journalist and his paper, *An Nahar,* sent him to the site to cover the events.

Afterward, Karim learned that those few short hours had been enough to plunge the country into civil war. People who had lived together peacefully until then turned to fighting in the streets. Barricades, shootings, overturned cars, rocket launches, hatred and destruction—that day had seen the birth of a spectacle that was to become sadly familiar over the years.

Karim grew up with the war. He suffered its effects without understanding its cause. Not that the experts themselves didn't get tangled in the threads of this unpredictable, often irrational war. No one could keep track anymore of its stops and starts, resumptions, reversals and surprises. Probably because of the complexity of the causes and the number of protagonists. Probably, too, because the local conflicts were compounded by foreign interference and agendas. And also because, like all wars, certain individuals and certain groups benefited from it.

In this war, the players' names are Christian, Muslim—Sunnite or Shiite—Druze, Palestinian, Syrian, Israeli. . . . Each party, each faction, has its armed militia. Each militia controls an area of the country or a part of Beirut. Alliances are made and unmade with each passing day or year; battles between militia are fierce. For years the city has been cut in two, divided down its center by the "Green Line," a long ribbon of ruins and desolation. To the east, the Christians. To the west, where Karim lives, the Muslims. By now there is no government left, no institutions, no electricity—or only for one or two hours a day—no running water. . . . Nothing but residents who gather by family, by building, by neighborhood, to survive the chaos in the middle of the urban jungle that is now Beirut. Its inhabitants have found small generators to produce electricity and dug wells in some neighborhoods.

Little by little, over the years, the people of Beirut have grown accustomed to this life, which from the outside seems inhuman. They've learned not to make plans, to live day to day, studying or working in spurts when conditions allow. They've learned to adapt their lives to the circumstances of war, to stay calm when shots ring out on the other side of the city or even in the next street. Among the ruins, in the heart of a steadily deteriorating city, life goes on, as elsewhere, with its laughter and tragedies, its loves and births, its dreams and disappointments.

But for three months, the situation has been intolerable. One bomb follows another at a frantic pace. Fear is everywhere. Above all, networks of neighbors are crumbling, the community is fraying. Beirut's inhabitants are fleeing the city like never before. Beginning in March when the bombing intensified, people who came from outside Beirut returned to their homes. For several weeks now, one after another, anyone who has the means is leaving the country, some for France, others for North Africa or America.

The case of the Nakad family is slightly different. A few days before the bombing resumed, Karim's parents, together with their youngest sons, Walid and Tarek, flew to Montreal in North America. Not because they sensed the coming danger, but simply to visit Karim's grandmother, who had taken refuge in Canada several years earlier and was scheduled for an operation. Her son and daughter-in-law wanted to be with her for the operation. Karim hadn't joined them because he was preparing for the first part of his baccalaureate exam and couldn't afford to miss any classes. His parents had finally agreed to leave him alone in Beirut.

"After all," his father said before leaving, "you're almost seventeen."

"And we'll only be gone three weeks," added his mother, not realizing the country's situation would deteriorate so badly that those three weeks would stretch into months, maybe even years.

Ironically, the lycée had been closed since March 14, the day bombs started to rain down furiously, and the exam was now the least of Karim's concerns.

March 14. He was on his way to the lycée with Béchir, his lifelong friend, when bombs exploded not far from them. Karim will always remember the chaos that ensued. People panicked, abandoning their cars in the middle of the street, creating huge traffic jams the police could do nothing about. Parents desperately searched for their children; children stood crying right in the middle of the street; shouts rang out everywhere.

Without much trouble, the boys managed to return to Béchir's house where they were welcomed with cries of relief and big hugs.

In no time, the telephone system was overloaded, so it took three days for Karim to get through to his parents, who were worried sick on the other side of the world. He tried to reassure them, saying that from a distance the situation always seems worse than it really is. Above all, he promised to stay with Béchir and his family until the danger was past.

For the first few days, the two boys had good intentions, cramming nonstop for their exam. Then, as the days passed and the bombs continued to fall, the two friends lost some of their zeal. After three weeks, they spent long hours playing backgammon or chess, philosophizing about life, death, love or, more and more frequently, about the respective merits of the girls they knew.

"I like Fatima and Raya," said Béchir. "They're good friends, and they don't take themselves too seriously."

For his part, Karim talked about Nada.

Nada! Just the sound of her name summoned up her tall silhouette, her hair so long and thick it was like a veil, her smile—tender or ironic depending on the day—her round hips, her heavy breasts that bounced when she ran. . . . All the details he found so exciting now but which had taken him so long to notice.

He'd known Nada forever, or almost. They'd both gone to the Lycée Abd-el-Kader in the heart of West Beirut since they were three. With the group of friends that made up their lycée crowd, they'd traced their first letters and learned their first words of French together. Like all the others, they'd played the same games and gone on the same outings and excursions organized by the lycée and the scouting movement. The two of them were bound by a healthy friendship like the one linking them to the rest of their group.

Karim had never felt the slightest bit aroused around Nada, no more than he was around any other girl for that matter, until that day last summer when, during a picnic, Nada leaned over to pour him some lemonade. As she did so, her blouse gaped open. Suddenly aware of her, Karim caught a glimpse of a pale band of skin, a hint of the curve of her breast.

It had lasted only a fraction of a second. Nada soon straightened up again, seemingly unaware of Karim's reaction. But that fraction of a second was enough to send Karim's senses and dreams skyrocketing.

The months that followed were one long, delicious

torment. He saw Nada as often as before, which was almost every day, in class or at friends' houses, but without ever receiving anything more than a smile or a sustained look from her. He would have liked to touch her, take her hand or kiss her, but he didn't dare, not in front of the others. As for seeing her alone, it was out of the question. Nada's parents were very strict and would never have let their daughter go out on a date.

At night in bed, Karim sometimes had trouble getting to sleep. He thought about Nada. He lingered over the image of her at the picnic, bared her breasts, her stomach. He imagined her naked body, smooth and creamy. He never dared push the wonderfully troubling images further and, with a vague sense of shame, hurriedly chased them from his mind.

At school, he tried not to show his interest in Nada. He confided only in Béchir.

"Well, do something," Béchir kept saying. "The role of bashful lover doesn't suit you in the least. Talk to her, write her a poem, take her flowers or chocolates, I don't know. But stop sighing and moaning every time you catch sight of her."

"I do not moan every time I look at her!"

"Yes, you do. You moan. To yourself, of course, but it's still a moan."

"No one can tell."

"That's what you think."

Béchir had almost managed to convince Karim to do something (a "something" as yet vague and undefined) when the bombing resumed, making any contact with Nada impossible.

"Just when you were going to go on the offensive," said Béchir despairingly.

After a while, his despair turned to exasperation

because Karim was spending more and more time talking about nothing but Nada, Nada, Nada.

"That's enough," he announced one April morning. "Tomorrow, for your birthday, we're going to go see Nada."

Karim was struck dumb with surprise.

"Well, what?" Béchir continued. "People go to the grocery store, to the drugstore, to the hospital. Why can't we go to Nada's? It'll get us outside. Every time we stick our noses out the door for two minutes, it's to kick a ball around, and I'm beginning to think I never want to see another ball again."

The next day, early on the morning of Karim's seventeenth birthday, the two friends went to Nada's.

"Can you imagine her expression when she sees us?"

Nada did, in fact, stare wide-eyed at the two characters who'd managed to reach her door and, with straight faces, were asking her to help them solve a "really tough" trigonometry problem.

Nada's mother frowned at the intrusion of the two boys into her daughter's bedroom, but even she had to admit that exceptional circumstances could justify unusual behavior that would be downright shocking in other circumstances.

"But leave the door open," she did think to add.

Between jokes and gales of laughter, Nada, Karim and Béchir talked about the trigonometry problem (for at least five seconds), exams, bombings, lycée, friends and the spring, which looked like it was going to be completely spoiled.

Then the boys had to leave.

"We have to be back at Béchir's before the bombing starts again," Karim felt he had to explain.

Béchir left the room first, after planting a big kiss on Nada's left cheek.

In turn, Karim approached Nada who held out her cheek.

"Oh, no! Not like that, not on my seventeenth birthday!" protested Karim in a tone he tried to keep light.

His lips touched hers.

Their kiss was brief and clumsy. His heart pounding, Karim tried to savor this first kiss . . . all the while keeping a watchful eye on the door where Mrs. Tabbara might appear at any moment.

Nada drew back almost immediately, blushing and slightly out of breath.

"My mother might see us."

On his way out, Karim murmured, "See you soon."

Nada didn't answer.

AFTER THAT, BÉCHIR AND KARIM went back to Nada's house several times. Nada wasn't surprised anymore to see the boys appear at dawn under the wildest pretexts.

Karim half regretted Béchir's presence, which meant he couldn't see Nada alone, but he knew her parents would have been more wary of a lone visitor than of two school friends. So he resigned himself to only seeing Nada in Béchir's company but couldn't help being even more impatient for the bombing to end and normal life to resume. A life where he could see Nada whenever he wanted and kiss her as often as he liked.

He tried to kiss her again during another visit, but Nada shied away.

"Hey! Not *another* birthday!" she protested, laughing as he bent toward her.

Karim told himself she was afraid of being seen and prayed even more fervently for the bombing to stop so that he could see Nada somewhere other than in an overcrowded apartment.

Unfortunately, the bombing didn't let up, residents

kept hiding out in their shelters or apartments, and more and more people decided to leave.

In early June, Béchir's family decided to leave as well, for Paris where a cousin could put them up.

"Are you sure you don't want to come with us, Karim?" Béchir's mother asked.

"No," he answered. "There's nothing for me in Paris."

"You'd be safe."

Suddenly, Karim was furious with all the "deserters."

"Safe, safe! That's all anyone can talk about. But what's the point of being safe if you don't even have a country left? Everyone leaving to be safe—nothing but cowards. Aren't you ashamed of deserting, of fleeing? The city's in ruins, and, yes, the country's in ruins, but at least it still exists. *Because of the people.* The day no one's left . . . the Syrians will set up shop for good in the East, the Israelis in the South, and . . . *pffft*, there'll be no Beirut anymore, no Lebanon, nothing!"

"The country is going to need the living when the time comes to rebuild," his friend's mother replied, "not the dead. There are already too many dead. And tell me, what is the glory in dying buried under the ruins or shot by a stray bullet? In dying *for nothing?*"

"I still think it's cowardly to leave."

But, of course, Béchir's parents didn't change their decision to leave Lebanon. As for Béchir, he was happy to finally have the opportunity to discover Paris.

"But I'll be back," he added on the day they left. "I'll be back with my engineering degree in my pocket, and I'll help rebuild the country. No matter what you say, I don't think it's more 'patriotic' to stay than to leave. I don't even think it's more heroic. In fact . . . are you sure you're staying out of patriotism, or is it for Nada's dark eyes?"

Karim was indignant.

"How can you say such a thing? It's disgusting."

But Béchir stopped him by placing a hand on his shoulder.

"Hey, don't get all worked up. Let's say it was just a joke. After all these years, it would be pretty dumb to part with a fight."

Karim calmed down. Yes, it would be dumb. Very dumb, actually.

The two boys hugged each other for a long while before separating.

NOW, NOTICING HOW HAPPY HE IS to be on his way to Nada, Karim thinks that maybe Béchir wasn't entirely wrong. Nada's eyes occupy his thoughts a great deal these days, more than the state of the city or the country. Nada's eyes, her body, her lips. Not to mention her smile, her lilting voice, her faintly sweet scent.

Karim is only a block from Nada's house. He smiles at the thought of finally seeing Nada alone today. Maybe he'll even be able to kiss her.

At this thought, Karim steps up his pace.

He turns the corner and comes to a full stop, frozen with horror.

The building in front of him is nothing but a smashed skeleton, blown to pieces, exposing in an obscurely obscene way the intimate interior of the ravaged apartments.

"Nada!"

Karim's cry is torn from his throat. The young girl's name vibrates a moment in the air before the silence snatches it away, a silence that only adds to his anguish.

He runs toward the building that his eyes scan in vain for signs of life. But no, how stupid of him, everyone must be hiding in the cellar, Nada as well as the others. That's where she must be this very moment, terrified maybe, but safe.

Karim searches among the debris for the entrance to the cellar. He digs feverishly, frustrated at finding nothing.

"Are you looking for something?"

The voice, behind him, gives him a start.

He turns around, stares speechless at the little girl standing in front of him, a baby perched on her hip, a gray cloth bag slung over her shoulder.

"You're Nada's sweetheart."

It is not a question but an observation.

Suddenly reassured, Karim recognizes the small face lifted to his, the huge eyes, the pointed chin. It's Nada's little sister, whom he's always seen from afar, in the school ground or, these past few weeks, at the far end of the Tabbara's living room. What is her name again?

"I'm Maha," announces the girl, who seems to have read his mind.

"Where's Nada? In the cellar?"

"There's no one in the cellar."

"Where's Nada?"

"She isn't there. They took her away."

"Who took her away? Where? Is she hurt?"

"No, she's dead."

Maha pronounces these words in an even, almost indifferent tone. But her pointed chin seems to tremble.

"I don't believe you," replies Karim abruptly. He doesn't want to believe her. He must not believe her.

The girl shrugs her shoulders and, turning on her heel, starts to walk away.

"No! Wait!" he cries out, suddenly panic-stricken. "Tell me . . . Tell me . . ."

He can't finish his sentence.

Maha has stopped walking. She waits for him to catch up with her before setting off again. Then in a clear, even voice, without looking at the tall boy walking at her side, she tells him.

"It was two days ago. During the night. The bombs were getting closer and closer. Every time, we thought we'd be hit. So everyone in the building went down to the cellar. Everyone, even the ones who usually didn't bother. My parents and Nada looked after helping our aunt Leila down while I took care of Jad. Jad, that's him," she adds, pointing with her chin to the baby now clinging to her neck. "He's six months old. My aunt Leila was old, fat and crippled. So to get her down from the fifth floor . . . Worse than moving a piano."

Maha breaks off long enough to anchor Jad, who keeps slipping down, more securely.

"I'd just gone into the shelter when the bomb fell. There was an awful noise, and everything started to shake. Three floors collapsed all at once. *Poof!* Underneath there was Aunt Leila, my parents . . . and Nada."

They stop in front of a relatively unscathed building. Sandbags are piled in front of the openings to the cellar. A heavy steel door protects the entrance to the shelter.

"There," concludes Maha, opening the door with a hard push. "You know it all now."

Mechanically, Karim follows her into the shelter. All of a sudden, he feels so tired. Dizzy almost. Empty of all emotion.

He's vaguely surprised at not feeling more despair. Nada is dead. Nada, whom he loves, is dead. He should be overwhelmed by grief, shaken with sobs. Instead, he's very calm. He feels like he's floating. Maybe Maha's strange detachment has rubbed off on him. Or else Nada's death still isn't real for him.

He does feel a panicky ache in his stomach and something like fear burrowing relentlessly inside him, but he's only aware of these sensations from a distance, as though they aren't happening to him but to someone else.

Suddenly, belligerent words penetrate the stupor that envelops him like a cocoon.

" . . . disgrace to see. Her parents' bodies not even cold yet, and she's already picking up boys. . . . You wouldn't have seen her sister doing such a thing, no not her. Nada was so polite. Such a shame, her death. Whereas this one . . . a bad seed. I've always said it. She's a bad seed. But the worse they are, the hardier they are as everyone knows. And—"

"But—" Karim tries to intervene.

"Be quiet," whispers Maha. "It's not worth it."

And she leads him to a corner while a young woman tries to calm the old woman still cursing Maha.

In spite of himself, Karim hears snatches of her tirade.

" . . . didn't even cry . . . her mother was right . . . come to no good . . . heartless . . . "

Maha, her eyes dry, her chin lifted in defiance, is busy feeding Jad.

Another rat's day begins, thinks Karim, who wonders what he's doing here among these strangers. Of course, it would have been different if Nada had been here. Nada!

Karim has to force himself to stifle the moan that rushes to his lips, to stop the tears that burn his eyes. He clenches his fists, squeezes his eyelids shut. Nada is dead. Dead. He will never see her again. He will never touch her again. He will never kiss her again. Never. Never. NEVER!

And he will never hold her naked body against his own.

Karim huddles down in his corner. He hides his face in his folded arms. He cries.

HE WAKES WITH A START, ashamed of having slept when Nada . . .

He shakes himself, looks around him.

About thirty people are crowded into the shelter. Some are playing cards, backgammon or chess, others are reading or knitting, still others are praying or talking quietly.

Maha, her back against the wall, looks like she's asleep. Her eyes are closed, her brow knit. In her arms, Jad sleeps soundly, his chin covered in drool.

Karim walks over to the backgammon players and watches the game for a minute.

"Do you want to play?" one of the players asks.

"Why not?"

And he sits down at one end of the board.

Casually, during the game, the others manage to slip in a question or two.

"Nice to have a new player. It's rare to see new faces in this hole. You a friend of the little one's?"

"No. I knew Nada. We were in the same class at the lycée."

The others nod their heads sadly.

"Ah, Nada. . . . Such a shame, her death. She was a nice girl. Always smiling, always friendly. And so pretty . . . "

"Not like her sister!" This interruption comes from the old woman who seems to hold such a grudge against Maha.

"You're exaggerating, Mrs. Farhat. Of course, she is more difficult, but—"

"A bad seed, I tell you! A bad seed that will come to no good! At least we'll soon be rid of her."

"Rid of her?" repeats Karim. "What do you mean?"

"In a few days, a Red Cross representative is supposed to come pick them up, her and her brother, to send them to an orphanage in France. They don't have any family left here, and since no one would be foolish enough to want to take *her* in . . . If it was just the baby, I'm not saying. But that girl . . . "

Mrs. Farhat seems about to embark on her favorite subject again, but one of the women nearby interrupts her.

"When the first-aid workers came for the injured and the dead the day before yesterday, they asked if there were any orphans. France has sent two hospital ships to evacuate the wounded and the orphans. They'll take them to Cyprus where the children will be sent to France by airplane. That's where Maha and Jad will go tomorrow or the next day."

"If they manage to take them away," points out one of the backgammon players. "Little Maha doesn't seem particularly pleased with the plan."

"Bah!" Mrs. Farhat breaks in. "They'll tie her up if they have to, but they'll take her away. That would be the limit if a snot-nosed little thing like her could defy the representatives of an official agency!"

"All the same, she seems dead set against it. She's determined to go instead to stay with the old man who used to work for them a while back. She said her parents had intended to send all three of them to him."

"And you believe that liar? Honestly, Mr. Khoury, you're so gullible!"

These words end the discussion while outside the first shells explode. The only bulb hanging from the ceiling sways dangerously but doesn't fall. The small generator set up in a corner still purrs away. A group of women raise their voices in prayer, joined by most of the shelter's occupants. "*Bismillah* . . . In the name of God, God of mercy, the Merciful . . . "

The monotonous hours drag on. The air is stifling with the odor of kerosene, sweat and tobacco. At times, songs can be heard or the sound of quickly suppressed tears. An old couple looks at pictures, reminiscing about evenings long gone. "You were wearing your gray suit, the one that made you look so distinguished." "And you, your green dress and diamond brooch." "No, my pearl necklace." "Do you think so?" "Yes, just look. And we ate . . . " In a corner, a woman downs valium after valium. Karim watches her, fascinated in spite of himself by the repetitive movement. He wonders if he shouldn't do something. The pills are a huge success in Beirut, sold over the counter in any drugstore. They're there for the taking as long as you pay.

Karim observes this underground life, so similar to life in the hole he shared with Béchir's family for weeks, so like the life in the shelter set up in his own building. All this time, he's aware of Maha, who's woken up and is now looking after the baby. She changes Jad's diaper, sets the dirty diaper aside to rinse out later, then takes a few steps, the baby in her arms. She speaks to no one, doesn't answer when she's spoken to, even when the words are kind. Karim doesn't understand her stubborn unpleasantness. If it wasn't for the glimmer of panic he detects deep in Maha's eyes, he'd say that Mrs. Farhat is right: the girl is hard and insensitive. But no doubt she's just terrified. And disoriented. Who wouldn't be?

He tries to comfort her a little, but his advances are no more welcome than the others'. Tough. Let her fend for herself. In any case, tomorrow at dawn, he's out of here. If he really has to lead a rat's life, at least he can lead it in his own hole.

A FURTIVE NOISE WAKES HIM. A mouse maybe? Or a rat, a real one? Rats have apparently been seen among the debris, even in broad daylight. Karim shivers in disgust as he tries in vain to make out something in the dark.

There's the noise again, a bit to his left. Someone—or "something"—is digging through the shelter's store of provisions.

Karim rises quietly and heads blindly in that direction. As his eyes adjust to the darkness, he soon realizes that the thief is human and not animal. Suddenly, the thief turns around, and with a muffled exclamation, Karim recognizes Maha.

"Hey . . . what are you doing?" he asks surprised.

"Shhh!" Maha whispers hastily. "You'll wake everyone."

"So? Why shouldn't I wake them all? Maybe it wouldn't be such a bad idea for them to see who's making off with their provisions. . . . Aren't you ashamed of yourself?"

Despite his threats, Karim keeps whispering. Maha picks up her bag and adds a round loaf of bread while looking Karim straight in the eye. Then, pulling him by the sleeve, she goes back to the corner where Jad sleeps. She gently picks up her brother, making sure not to wake him, then heads for the exit, still followed by Karim.

Once outside, Karim lets loose the questions he's been dying to ask.

"Would you please tell me what you're up to? Stealing food, sneaking out in the middle of the night . . . Are you crazy or what?"

Maha is silent for a few seconds. Then she takes a big breath and, her eyes intent on Karim's, says, "I'm going to Chlifa. You can come if you want."

Taken aback, Karim stammers out the first thing that comes to mind.

"Chlifa. Where's Chlifa?"

"On the other side of the mountains, in the Beqaa, not too far from Baalbek."

This time, Karim can't think of anything to say. And when he finally finds his voice, he says, "You're crazy. You are totally crazy."

In the dark, Maha's eyes send off sparks. Karim imagines, more than sees, her small chin raised in anger.

"Oh, yes? I'm crazy? We'll see about that."

And grasping Jad tighter to her, her cloth bag slung across her shoulder, Maha sets off. After several steps, she turns around.

"And when I get there, to Chlifa, I'll send you a postcard. If the bombs haven't got you by then."

She resumes walking with a determined gait, plunging into the Beirut night, the deadly Beirut night, crisscrossed with shells, punctuated by rocket launches, riddled with traps.

"Damn!" Karim exclaims before setting off in pursuit. All he can think of is getting her back to the shelter willingly or by force before something happens to her. He'll knock her out if he has to or drag her by her long braids, but he is going to take her back. She's crazy, really crazy. If only she were alone in her craziness . . . but no, she has to drag the baby along with her. . . .

He has no trouble catching up to her. As soon as he's at her side, he grabs her arm and pulls her roughly into the limited shelter offered by a still-standing section of wall and a heap of debris.

When Karim lets go, she sets Jad down on the ground before turning to him, her fists clenched, her eyes flashing.

"I don't have to take orders from you, do you hear

me? I want to go to Chlifa, and I *am* going to Chlifa whether you like it or not. You're not my father or my brother, and just because you kissed my sister doesn't mean you have any rights over me, understood? So go hide in your hole. I'm leaving for Chlifa."

"You don't even know how to get there."

"Oh, no? Wait. You'll see."

Changing his tactics, Karim decides he won't take Maha back by force. Instead, he'll prove to her that her plan doesn't make sense. He'll show her one argument at a time that she has no chance of making it to Chlifa, even if she does manage to get out of Beirut, which is far from certain.

"Look!" exclaims Maha who, after digging around in her big bag, has just pulled out a map of Lebanon.

It's a worn, crumpled map, ripped along the folds and missing a big chunk from the bottom left-hand corner. Tyre is missing and so is the whole southern portion of the country. Sidon is just barely visible. Karim thinks that the map may very well reflect reality. Today's reality or tomorrow's. All it would take would be to keep tearing off chunks. The South to the Israelis. The North and East to the Syrians. Little by little, you'd keep tearing off bits of the map, eating away at the edges of the country until nothing was left but Beirut pressed up against the sea. Nothing would be left of Beirut but ruins that would eventually vanish as well, swept away by the wind.

"You see," continues Maha, "here's Beirut. Chlifa is there at the foot of Mount Lebanon. I just have to head east, along this road here that leads to Zahlé, then—"

" . . . then die a dozen deaths before taking a dozen steps. You don't seem to realize that the road you're talking about goes right through the Christian strong-hold, right through the region most heavily bombed by the Syrians. If you think life in West Beirut isn't much fun these days, my little one, it's nothing compared to what's happening over there."

"I'm not *your* little one."

"Okay. Little one, then. In fact, that's the second problem. Even if you found a fairly safe route, do you really think the militia or the Syrian soldiers are going to let two children head off like that onto the roads? Do you really think that at every roadblock, after they search you and ask the usual questions, they're going to say, "Oh! This is perfect! Of course, you can pass. After all, what could be more normal than little ten-year-old girls walking around with babies in their arms in the middle of a war. . . ."

"I'm twelve!"

Karim can't help looking Maha up and down from head to toe. His disbelief must show because, flushed with anger and perhaps shame, she quickly adds as she pulls herself up and sticks out her chest, "What's more, I'm going to be thirteen in September. I was born in 1976. Unfortunately, I can't show you my birth certificate. Unless you feel like rummaging through the ruins back there."

"That's strange. . . . It seems to me that Nada at twelve . . . "

"Oh, right! Nada at twelve had breasts and hips and huge sparkling eyes. A real little woman! So what?"

Maha screams the last words. Karim, feeling uncomfortable, tries to calm her down.

"Listen, it doesn't matter. I suppose every girl develops differently. After all, you're not like Nada in any other way either."

"Really, you noticed. . . ."

She tries to sound sarcastic, but her voice trembles a bit. Karim remembers Mrs. Farhat's words, her comparisons that hurt Maha, and he regrets having raised what is obviously a very touchy subject. And anyway, how did he get caught up in this kind of discussion? He feels he's strayed considerably from the reasonable demonstration of logic meant to make Maha see the impossibility of her plan. He tries to get back on track.

"Plus, you're not equipped to make a hundred-and-fifty-kilometer trip on foot with a baby in your arms."

"It isn't a hundred and fifty kilometers. It's barely eighty."

Karim explodes.

"Would you quit quibbling about details! What does it matter if you're ten or twelve, or if Chlifa is eighty or one hundred and fifty kilometers away? It's a long way. There's a war on. You're young. You're not equipped. You can't do it. *Quod erat demonstrandum.*"

"*Quod* what?"

Suddenly, Karim feels awfully tired.

"Nothing, nothing."

He holds his hand out for the cloth bag that Maha still has slung over her shoulder. Without a word, Maha passes it to him. He opens the bag, empties its contents on the ground. A flashlight rolls at his feet. He takes it, turns it on, shines its beam on the objects spread out before him. A tiny, drooping teddy bear. A loaf of bread. A jar of peach jam. Two apples. Four oranges. Matches. Powdered milk. A small pan. A glass globe filled with stars that sparkle when it's shaken. A red comb. Strips of cloth. He looks at Maha questioningly. "Spare diapers," she explains. "I've got four of them. If I wash them as I go and leave them out to dry, they should do." A red sweater for her. A yellow sweater for the baby. A book of nursery rhymes from which a picture drops. Karim picks up the picture and stares for a long time at the smiling faces looking out at him. Nada, Maha and their parents gathered around the new baby sleeping with his fists clenched. The picture of a happy family. The picture of Nada happy.

"I don't have anything else," murmurs Maha at his side. "I don't have anyone else. Except for him," she adds fervently as she bends over to pick Jad up again. "And I won't let anyone take him away from me."

"No one said they would."

"Mrs. Farhat said they'd separate us in France."

"You know Mrs. Farhat hates you. She'd say anything to hurt you."

"Can you swear to me that they wouldn't separate us?"

"Well—"

Maha interrupts him.

"You don't know. You don't know anymore than I do. Me, I can't run that risk, do you understand? You said I was quibbling over details and that what's important is whether I'm well equipped and what route I'll take. You haven't understood a thing. Not a thing. What's important is that I don't have anything left to lose. Except Jad. You say we'll be killed before we reach Chlifa. That's a shame, but that's the way it is. Two deaths more or less won't make much of a difference."

"You've no right to say such a thing! It's . . . it's blasphemy."

"No, it's the truth. Oh, don't worry. I don't especially want to die, and I'm not going to throw myself into a bullet's path on purpose. . . . But I'd rather die with Jad than live without him. See, he's all I have left. And I'm all he has left. So . . . "

She takes the picture from Karim's hands, slips it between the pages of the little book, then starts to put the things spread out on the ground back into the bag.

When she's through, she sets the bag comfortably on

her shoulder, anchors Jad on her left hip and, without a glance at Karim, sets off again into the night.

His eyes fixed on the ground, Karim listens to the sound of her retreating steps. He hears the grinding of sand under her shoes. He hears her bump against something and muffle a small cry of pain.

Then, without further hesitation, he runs after her.

"I'm going with you," he calls out, slightly out of breath as he draws near. "I think I know how we could get out of the city. And then . . . "

He stops when he realizes Maha has stopped and that she's staring at him with an expression he can't decipher.

"And then . . . " she says in a neutral voice.

"And then, for starters, pass me Jad. We can take turns carrying him. It won't be as tiring that way."

Maha keeps staring at his face in the dark.

"Is it true? Is it really true?" she finally asks hesitantly, as though she doesn't dare believe it.

"Looks like it."

A slow smile creeps over the young girl's features. A smile that transforms her small, pointed face and makes her eyes shine. Eyes that are unusually large in the dark.

"Well, then . . . en route, fellow traveler!"

And she holds out Jad, who's just woken up and seems to accept the change in bearer quite philosophically.

Several hours later, while they wait for the best time to cross the Green Line, Karim wonders why, against all reason, he decided to join Maha in her crazy undertaking.

Out of a need to protect Nada's sister and brother? The instinctive reaction of a fearless knight beyond reproach? Although perhaps the easiest explanation, it only partially satisfies him.

To his great surprise, he suddenly realizes that what made him decide to leave was precisely the very craziness of this journey to the other side of Mount Lebanon, a journey that's the exact opposite of the life he's been leading for months now. The opposite of fear, underground hideaways, inaction. Suddenly, Karim feels the desire to live, not vegetate.

And there's no one left to keep him in Beirut.

"BY THE WAY, what are you going to do in Chlifa?"

Maha gives a small, amused laugh.

"I was beginning to wonder if you'd ever ask me that."

"So?"

"So, we're going to old Elias's house."

"And who's old Elias?" insists Karim, who, unlike Maha, is hard pressed to find anything amusing about this guessing game where the answers are doled out in driblets.

"A man who used to work for my parents in their grocery store. His wife, Zahra, looked after us during the day. She was huge, covered in hair and warts . . . and I adored her. She stuffed us with candy and pastry, Nada and me. Elias and Zahra went back to their village, Chlifa, three or four years ago. My parents had been planning to send us there for a while when . . . when the building collapsed. But that won't stop me from going anyway."

Why not? thinks Karim, who's beginning to get used to the idea of crossing part of the country despite the bombs and the obstacles separating them from their goal.

Chlifa is on the east slope of Mount Lebanon, on the other side of the high mountain range stretching from north to south that forms the country's spine. In fact, the country as a whole is named after those same mountains. The word "Lebanon," *Loubnân* in Arabic, comes from the word *leben,* which means "milk" or "white," and originally referred to the high, snow-covered peaks before it came to be used for the whole country. The village of Chlifa lies between the mountains and the Beqaa Valley, the long plain that stretches from Mount Lebanon to the Anti-Lebanon, another mountain range parallel to the first that marks, to the east, the border with Syria.

On Maha's map, nothing looks easier than traveling to Chlifa. Unfortunately, the map doesn't show combat zones, roads that have been cut off or the militia's or soldiers' roadblocks. No more than it shows who controls the areas they'll have to cross. Karim seems to remember that there are a lot of Christians where they're going, and that the Beqaa itself is divided between the Syrians and Hezbollah fanatics. Maybe the Iranians, too. Karim regrets that he isn't more up to date on the situation.

But before confronting the mountain and the Beqaa Valley, they have to face a more immediate problem—crossing over to East Beirut.

To exit Beirut to the north—unless they want to swim across Saint George Bay—they first have to make a small detour eastward, into the Christian zone, to cross the famous Green Line that for years has separated West Beirut from East Beirut, the Muslim sector from the Christian sector. The Green Line, some fifteen kilometers long, is now nothing more than a heap of ruins and debris serving as a buffer zone between the two camps. Although there are a few crossing points between East and West—including the Mathaf crossing that Karim and Maha intend to take—it's become particularly dangerous to cross from one side to the other, especially over the last three months. Snipers have no qualms about shooting anything that moves in this deserted space strewn with debris and overtaken by wild grasses, which earned it the almost poetic name *Green* Line. However, Karim and Maha have no choice. They have to take their chances crossing to the Christian side.

"READY?" Karim finally asks as the sky takes on a lighter hue and the noise of fighting dies down.

Maha nods.

"All right, let's go."

He stands, takes Jad back in his arms and with Maha at his side advances toward the crossing, his heart beating quickly, his mind hesitating between the fear of failure and the joy of experiencing something new, different, exhilarating.

Please let it work, Karim says over and over to himself. Just let it work. The slightest hitch could ruin everything.

During the night, Maha and he spent quite awhile focusing on a question of paramount importance: would it be better to come right out and reveal the purpose of their trip when the militia interrogated them, or would it be wiser to say as little as possible? Karim was in favor of speaking out while Maha thought it would be safer to say nothing.

"How're we going to justify crossing over to the East?"

"We'll say we're going to see one of our uncles, our mother's brother."

"'Our' mother?"

"Uh-huh. We're better off pretending to be brother and sister. That way we won't arouse any suspicion."

Suspicion of what? Karim almost asked. Do you really think they might take us for spies or eloping lovers? But he kept quiet. Maha seemed quite touchy on certain subjects, and this was not a good time to provoke an angry outburst.

"WHAT'S YOUR UNCLE'S NAME?" the militiaman is asking suspiciously. "And where does he live?"

Karim can feel Maha stiffen beside him and senses she's about to give a name, any name, to get the interrogation over with as quickly as possible. He also senses that the militiaman is not the kind to be satisfied with a made-up name and that he might ask other awkward questions.

"His name is Antoine Milad," Karim interjects, giving the name of one of his father's friends. "I don't know his exact address, but he's a journalist with *El-Amal.* With that information, we should be able to find him easily enough."

Karim hopes the militiaman will let them by without any trouble so they can continue on their way as planned, through the Christian sector, then over the Nahr Beirut, the river that marks the city's administrative limits. It doesn't matter that they don't know that sector of the city. They just have to head generally northeast, and they're bound to end up more or less where they want to.

But the militiaman doesn't let them off that easily.

"Do you know how to find the newspaper's offices?"

"We'll figure it out."

"Follow me."

Soon it's obvious the man won't let them into the Christian side before he's sure that they are who they say they are and that they're really going to see their uncle who's a journalist.

"Do we look that dangerous?" jokes Karim, pointing to Maha and the baby.

"We've seen stranger disguises than that. Wait here."

The militiaman leaves them in a bare, tiny room where they wait for what seems like hours.

"What do you think they're doing?" asks Maha after a while.

"They're looking for Antoine Milad, I guess."

"Does he really exist?"

"Uh-huh."

Mockingly, Karim answers Maha the same way she did earlier on. In driblets.

"And who's Antoine Milad?"

"A friend of my father's."

"A Christian?"

"Yes, of course."

"Do you trust him?"

"We don't have much choice."

"But do you trust him?" Maha insists.

"Yes."

"What happens if they find him?"

"We'll leave with him."

"And if he tells them he doesn't have any nieces or nephews?"

"He won't say that."

"And if they don't find him?"

"Their only choice will be to let us go anyway."

To tell the truth, Karim is puzzled and not nearly as confident as he looks. Why has the militiaman insisted on keeping them under surveillance? Because he doesn't believe their story? Doesn't trust them? To help them? To protect them? To make sure they end up in good hands? Nothing in the man's attitude points to one explanation more than the other. But, whatever his reason, the special attention bothers Karim. What will happen to them? Will they have to go back to the Muslim sector? Will they stay trapped on the boundary between the two camps? He's heard of unexplained disappearances, kidnappings, summary executions. It doesn't take much to start imagining the worst atrocities when you don't understand what's going on.

"We'll have to find a way of heating up some water," announces Maha after a while. "Jad's going to want his bottle soon."

A bottle! As if the situation wasn't already complicated enough, Karim thinks to himself. I really have stumbled onto a wasps' nest. Playing tourist in wartime with a ravenous baby and an unpredictable girl.

"Take Jad, and I'll go look for a hot plate," Maha says.

"No!" Karim is quick to reply. "You stay here with your brother. I'll go look for a solution to the milk problem."

"You afraid of being alone with a baby?"

Maha sounds somewhat scornful.

"Afraid? Of course not! What an idea! I . . . it's just that I think it's better this way."

"Is that according to the Prophet?"

Karim feels he's on dangerous ground. He has no desire to get involved in a discussion that could become either theological or feminist. So he carefully refrains from speaking as he leaves the room to look for some hot water. As soon as he steps outside the door, Jad starts to howl, and Karim congratulates himself on having gotten away in the nick of time.

"Here they are," a voice announces a little later. They

had finally dozed off once Jad was fed and changed, and his diaper was rinsed as well as could be.

Instantly awake, Karim stares at the man standing in the doorframe. Yes, this is his father's friend whom he's seen before in pictures. The man has aged, his body thickened and his hair turned gray, but Karim recognizes his tall frame, his Roman nose, the cigarette in the corner of his mouth.

"Uncle Antoine!" he cries out before the man says anything that might give them away. "My parents told me so much about you."

The man's gaze settles on him, and a glimmer of understanding flashes in his eyes.

"Karim? It is Karim, isn't it? It's incredible how much you look like Salim! I feel like I've gone back twenty-five years. Karim . . . the son of my dear Agnès and my friend Salim. But tell me, the others, they are . . . "

"Maha and Jad, yes," Karim adds quickly.

Karim feels relieved. Antoine Milad is here; he's grasped the situation in no time; he won't betray them.

"Since our parents' death, you're the only family we have left. Mother always said, 'If anything ever happens to us, go to my brother Antoine. He'll look after you.'"

The man standing before them sways as though in shock. He closes his eyes and stammers, "Dead? Agnès and Salim dead! How awful. Oh, God! How awful!"

The militiaman is watching the whole scene from where he stands off to the side.

"All right, if everything's in order, you may leave."

"AND NOW," SAYS ANTOINE MILAD once they've all squeezed into his car, a green car that has obviously seen better days, "if you wouldn't mind telling me what's going on. . . . To begin with, what's this about

Salim and Agnès being dead? I spoke to Salim two days ago on the phone. He was in Montreal, safe from any danger. In fact, his greatest worry is knowing you're in Beirut alone, young man. He's afraid something might happen to you. What would he think if he knew you get your kicks crossing the Green Line and wandering through the city with a little girl and a baby. . . ."

"I'm not a little girl!" protests Maha crossly.

Antoine Milad casts a quick glance her way.

"Maybe not," he says. "Let's say I'm reserving judgment for the time being. But I would very much like to know where you come into the picture and what the three of you are doing here."

"Well . . . " Karim begins slowly.

"Then again, no," Antoine Milad breaks in. "Don't start what's bound to be a highly convoluted explanation just yet. Let's wait until we get to my house. Once I've had one or two good strong cups of coffee, I'll have a chance of understanding better."

"WOULD YOU LIKE SOME COFFEE, children? Or some orange juice? That is, if I have orange juice. Let's see. . . . Yes, well. It may not be as fresh as it could be, but it looks about the right color. And the baby, what about him? What does a baby drink? Milk? I'm not sure I have any milk. Cream, yes, a bit, but milk?"

"He had his bottle not long ago," says Maha. "And anyway, I have powdered milk for him. I just have to boil some water, cool it down, then stir the powder in."

"Long live progress. So, since the matter of milk is settled, how about we start all over? Your name is Maya, and his is Jad."

"Maha," she corrects him.

"Sorry, Maha. Now, Maha, may I know who you are exactly and where you fit into the picture? Agnès and

Salim never had a daughter, as far as I know, and the baby of the family must be six years old by now."

"Eight," points out Karim.

"Eight, then. One more reason why he can't be this little tyke, who seems very young. But let's get back to—"

Maha interrupts him midstream.

"I'm going to Chlifa with Jad. Karim is coming with us. His parents didn't die. Our parents are the ones who died."

For once, Antoine Milad seems speechless.

He pours himself a thick, steaming coffee, serves them some orange juice, lights a cigarette.

Then he clears his throat two or three times before speaking.

"I'm very sorry about your parents. It's so tragic, tragic and absurd, all these deaths, all these pointless, anonymous deaths, bereft of meaning. . . ."

He shakes his head helplessly.

"And me?" he asks after emptying half his cup. "What can I do to help you?"

"Nothing," Maha replies curtly. "We never even meant to get you involved. If it hadn't been for that militiaman going beyond the call of duty, we'd already be long gone. In fact, we'll be leaving again as soon as we've finished our orange juice."

"Whoa there! What did I say to deserve that reaction? Leave right away? You can't mean it. You're dead tired. You can't even keep your eyes open, and a few hours sleep wouldn't hurt Karim either. Besides, where would you go? The bombing's going to start up again any minute."

"Don't worry about us. We know how to take care of ourselves," Maha declares proudly. "We're tough, you know."

But her whole body betrays her words. She's frail, pale, with dark shadows under her eyes. And, as Antoine

Milad said, she's having trouble keeping her eyes open. Karim thinks to himself that it won't do them much good if she drops from exhaustion after half an hour. So he decides to say something.

"He's right, Maha. Let's rest for a few hours, then leave."

Maha hesitates. Obviously, she doesn't trust Milad. She drags Karim into a corner.

"Promise we'll leave right after?"

"Promise."

"Promise you won't let him convince you that we're nothing but two flighty kids with a half-baked plan?"

"It's true our plan's half-baked. But that won't stop us from leaving."

"Promise?" Maha insists.

"I promise."

"On the head of Mohammed, Jesus and all the prophets?"

"I promise. That should be enough. No need to swear."

Maha lifts her eyes to the ceiling.

"You're just like Nada. She thought everything was swearing."

Nada. That blow to his heart again. Suddenly, Karim feels exhausted. No doubt about it, all this arguing and bickering with Maha is draining.

"Come on. Bedtime, little one."

"Quit calling me little one."

"So bedtime, grandma. On the double."

Maha sticks her tongue out at him.

The afternoon is drawing to a close. In front of his old Remington typewriter, Antoine Milad sits chewing on a cigarette while he thinks about how to finish his article. An article that will probably never be published because newspapers are appearing only sporadically, but asking Antoine Milad to stop writing is like asking him to stop breathing . . . or smoking.

"What's this?" Maha asks suddenly behind him.

She's barefoot, which is why he didn't hear her footsteps on the tiles. Her braids are partly undone, and she still seems warm from sleep. She looks vulnerable, the way people do when they just wake up, and once again the journalist curses this war that makes children orphans.

Maha is absorbed, contemplating a postcard pinned to the wall. An elegantly clad woman in a long, golden gown is playing a miniature organ set on a stand draped with a tapestry. On the other side of the organ, a second, smaller woman is holding something, maybe a book of music or a bellows. Around the two women stand a lion, a unicorn and several small animals. They're on a little island of greenery like a soft, soft carpet sown with many colorful flowers. The background of the painting is red; it, too, is strewn with flowers and leafy branches.

"It's one of the Lady with the Unicorn tapestries. Do you like it?"

Maha nods without saying a word. She hasn't taken her eyes off the picture that seems to fascinate her. She examines it in minute detail. The faintly odd hat the woman is wearing. Her gown decorated with jewels. Her pale, pensive beauty. The fruit and flowers in the scenery. The little rabbits. The fox. And the unicorn. A sorrowful-looking unicorn, its head turned in the direction of the two women, its long twisted horn, its slightly tilted eye . . .

"Several tapestries in the same series are on exhibit at the Musée de Cluny in Paris. They were woven more than five hundred years ago."

Maha keeps staring at the image as though she wants to engrave its every detail in her memory. After a long pause, she begins speaking in a soft, pensive voice, a voice the journalist hasn't heard her use before.

"It's like a dream. As if I've always been looking for a lost dream without ever finding it. And then, all of a sudden, the dream's in front of me, even more beautiful than I imagined. A dream where people and animals can stand quietly together in a field of flowers *without fear.* One day, I'm going to live in a place just like that."

She turns her head to look at the journalist.

"And that day," she says in a fervent voice, "that day, there will be peace."

Antoine Milad doesn't have the heart to tell her that peace isn't always such a paradise, that it is rarely pure and untainted.

He pulls lightly on one of Maha's braids to shake the emotion that has him by the throat.

"The next time I meet up with a unicorn, little one, I promise to bring it back to you."

Maha gives a half-smile, then shakes her head.

"No. Unicorns are fragile. They have to be left free."

"What on earth are you talking about?" Karim asks, surprised. He has just entered the room and can't see where unicorns figure among their present concerns.

"Unicorns and peace."

"In other words, illusions, figments of the imagination," says Karim.

"They are not figments of the imagination," Maha retorts vehemently. "They exist. Just because the war's been going on for fourteen years doesn't mean that peace doesn't exist. Before . . . "

"Oh, no!" moans Karim. "You're not going to talk about *before*, too, are you? Before, before, before. . . . That's all older people talk about. *Before* was heaven on earth. Lebanon was the 'Switzerland of the Middle East.' Beirut was an oasis of peace, a meeting place, a haven for tolerance, intellectual stimulation and economic prosperity. Everyone loved his neighbor. Races and religions lived side by side in an atmosphere of harmony and respect. And all that in the most beautiful country in the world—the ever-present sea, the mountains on our doorstep, an enchanting climate, breathtaking vistas, archeological and tourist sites by the spadeful, a quality of light praised by poets and artists past and present. . . . The problem is that we who are young never knew *before*. We've only known *after*, which is not a pretty sight. What I don't understand is how such a paradise turned into such a hell so quickly."

Karim looks at Antoine Milad as if he holds him personally responsible for the war and its atrocities.

Milad runs both hands through his hair before lighting yet another cigarette.

"There's no simple answer," he finally replies in a serious tone. "If there were, everything would have been settled quickly, and we wouldn't be mired in this endless war. But one thing's certain—the paradise that almost everyone waxes nostalgic over was only an illusion reserved for the rich, the cultivated Beirut elite, whether Christian or Muslim. Under the surface of their illusion, problems abounded that eventually had to erupt. There wasn't just tension between Christians and Muslims. There was tension between rich and poor, the right and the left, people from the cities and people from the country. . . . There was friction pretty well everywhere on all sides. And with the eruption of the first events, everything fell apart. However, it wasn't totally unforeseeable."

"But everyone seems to want things to be the way they used to be."

"When the war first started, during the early years, yes, I think a lot of people were just waiting for things to go back to the way they were. As if the war was just an interruption in the course of their lives. As if time was on hold. They awaited war's end, thinking they could take up where they'd left off. Then, as time went by, something happened to change that overly simplistic view. One death too many. An especially rude awakening one morning. People keep talking about before, all the while knowing that things will never be the same again. That we are using up our lives each and every day in the heart of this conflict. That the future began a long time ago. That . . . "

Milad stops and looks at his hands. Then he stares into Karim's eyes.

"You're right to resent the older generation, to hold a grudge against us. You young people, you don't even have the good memories. Your view is limited to the horror or—worse yet—the banality of war. We've passed on to you a world without hope, without a future. All that's left for you is death, whether violent or slow. Even the people fighting don't know why they do it most of the time."

"Maybe to prove they exist," murmurs Karim, "to have the satisfaction of doing something. There are days when everything seems so unreal."

Milad rolls his cigarette between his fingers before continuing.

"For a long time, I thought it was important to stay, to resist by staying put," he says, "to show the world that we are here and that we won't disappear without making ourselves heard. Now I don't know anymore. In any case, the world's forgotten about us. Wars that go on forever don't interest anyone. We still make the headlines every once in a while when something really 'juicy' happens. When the 241 American marines and 88 French paratroopers were killed. When there are lots of fatalities and lots of blood all at once. When it makes for gripping images to show on TV. The rest of the time, we're forgotten. Under conditions like that, what does it matter anymore whether we stay or go?"

Karim doesn't answer. He remembers what he told Béchir's mother. He remembers how angry he was with the deserters, the cowards, the traitors. He can't feel anger anymore.

Maha lost interest in the conversation a while back. She's walking around the room looking at books, posters, the odd collection of objects littering the journalist's desk. Trinkets, drawings, a pack of matches, an old menu with part of a sentence scribbled on the back, a nail trimmer, a package of cookies, a half-dozen not-so-clean ashtrays.

"Are you sure you don't want to stay here with me?" Antoine Milad suddenly asks. "Or that you don't want me to move heaven and earth to send you to Montreal to Karim's parents? It's not that I want to interfere, but I do feel kind of responsible for you, and I'm worried about letting you leave without really knowing what you mean to do. You, little one, where did you say you were going?"

Maha keeps quiet for a minute. Then, after looking to Karim, she tells the journalist their destination.

"Chlifa, Chlifa. That name rings a bell. Isn't it in the direction of the Beqaa?"

"Uh-huh. Not far from Baalbek."

"I've been there before, a long time ago. With your

father," he adds for Karim's benefit. "For three months one summer, we traveled the country on foot. Must have been 1965, yes that's it, 1965. We were eighteen years old and out to discover the world. It feels like centuries ago. . . . I've got pictures of that summer that I should be able to dig up without too much trouble. Are you interested?"

"Yes," says Karim, curious to discover a side of his father he doesn't know.

Maha doesn't answer. After the picture viewing session, then what? Time to bring out the baby toys? A game of backgammon? A visit to Antoine Milad's aging mother? At this rate, it could take them forever to get to Chlifa.

But the picture viewing session turns out to be more rewarding than Maha could have imagined because, along with the pictures, they find maps, travel guides, the diary Antoine Milad kept for three months . . . and memories.

"Good lord!" the journalist suddenly exclaims. "I know the best route for you to take to Chlifa! Why didn't I think of it sooner? Children, what would you say to a real trip through the wilderness, far from roads and their danger? I know a mountain path that links the western and eastern slopes of Mount Lebanon . . . and leads to within a few kilometers of Chlifa. That way, you can avoid the roads as well as the area immediately surrounding Baalbek, which isn't too safe these days. In fact, the *whole* Beqaa Valley is dangerous . . . and if you take the route I'm thinking of, you'll avoid the valley on your way to Chlifa."

Right then and there he begins to trace their route on a large-scale map.

Karim and Maha exchange puzzled looks. Karim is torn between irritation at having this man decide everything for them without even asking their opinion

78

and excitement at the thought of an expedition in the wilderness. Not to mention being able to relive his father's adventure of almost twenty-five years ago. This would be one way of feeling closer to him, of bridging the years and the continents.

"Your best bet is to avoid all roads. Here, you could follow the course of the Nahr el-Kelb, over there, the base of the mountain massif. . . . You only need enough food for three or four days, let's say five to be on the safe side. Which shouldn't be a problem. . . ."

Antoine Milad's enthusiasm is contagious, and soon Karim and Maha, all reservations forgotten, are caught up in the excitement of their new adventure.

"Children, if it weren't for my aging mother whom I really can't abandon right now, I do think I'd go with you. In any case . . . I'll have to make do with taking you on the first part of your trip. Tomorrow morning at dawn, I'll drive you as far as the Nahr el-Kelb. That'll probably be the trickiest part of the trip. Leaving Beirut, getting past all the barricades, passing through several towns. . . . You'll never manage it on your own or at least not without an incredible amount of trouble. It's better for you to be with me. We'll keep the uncle story, and I'll say that I'm driving you to Juniyah to a cousin's house. Now in the meantime, I'll look after getting some supplies and warm clothes together for you. Mountain nights can be cold in June. As for you two, bedtime."

"Again!" Karim and Maha protest in chorus.

"You can never rest up too much before this kind of expedition."

Dawn once more. A pale dawn, but one full of promise. Jad woke up just as the fighting was dying down, and immediately, quickly and silently, Maha started to look after him. Karim notices he's watching her precise, efficient gestures with great interest.

"Did Nada look after Jad, too?" he asks suddenly, realizing with a feeling bordering on panic that Nada's memory is beginning to fade in his mind and that he'll never know certain things about her.

"Not much, no," Maha replies curtly. "Seems that the smell of milk and poo turned her stomach. So looking after a baby . . . "

She leaves her sentence unfinished, checks the temperature of the milk she's just heated up, props Jad in the crook of her arm and holds the bottle up to the baby's eager mouth. Then she looks over at Karim, who's still watching her.

"Maybe you didn't know Nada as well as you think. I mean . . . "

Karim doesn't let her finish.

"I'm going to check on the gear."

He leaves. He isn't ready to hear about Nada. Not yet. Maybe never.

CANVAS KNAPSACKS, A SMALL TENT, a burner, utensils, blankets, a compass, cans of tuna, packages of soup, maps, powdered milk for the baby, soap, toothpaste, a big package of dates . . . As he discovers what Antoine Milad has managed to scrounge up, Karim bursts out laughing.

"Looks more like we're scouts off to camp than refugees on the run, don't you think?"

"If only that were the case. . . . But before scout camp, you're going to have to run the obstacle course—getting out of the city. Are Maha and Jad ready?"

"Uh-huh," answers Maha at the door. "I just have to put on Jad's booties."

Once the baggage is in place, they settle into Milad's car and take off in the direction of the port.

"I just hope that Charles Hélou Avenue's still open to traffic," Milad grumbles between his teeth. "You certainly can't get in a rut in this city. One morning you take one street; the next day, it's disappeared under the rubble or it's cut off by the gaping hole left by a bomb. Every day you find new barricades, new detours, new burned-out shells of cars. Streets we once thought were safe are now nothing less than shooting ranges. Even the shortest trip is full of danger and suspense."

Karim is taking it all in, the streets he's never seen before and the rare pedestrians hurrying along them. Like yesterday, he's struck by the similarities to West Beirut. Similar in its dilapidation, its desolation. At the same time though, he feels disoriented. He can't get his bearings. His mind knows which way the car is going, but it doesn't feel right.

"What's it going to be like when we're in totally unknown territory?" he wonders a bit apprehensively. "No, not totally unknown," he corrects himself in the next breath. "Not by my father."

He's seized by a new emotion. A mixture of nostalgia, love, pride and mushy sentimentalism. Following in his father's footsteps, walking along the paths of memory, erasing time and space . . . He tries to find the words to describe what this crossing, this pilgrimage represents for him. But he can't. The words, the feelings remain just outside his grasp. Which makes him sad somehow.

But soon his thoughts turn to the first real obstacle on their route—a barricade put up by the militia. A few cars are already in line ahead of them. They have to wait.

Militiamen interrogate the drivers one after another, check their papers, rummage through their trunks. The ritual is the same on both sides of the Green Line. Courtesy seems as foreign to one side as to the other.

Their turn has come. Milad shows his papers and his journalist's card that usually opens doors and speeds up formalities. Then he motions to his passengers.

"My niece and nephews. Their parents died three days ago, and I've decided to drive them to Juniyah to a cousin's place."

The militiamen glance at the silent teenagers and the baby snoring softly as he sleeps.

"Go ahead. But don't take the viaduct. It isn't safe. Take En-Nahr Street instead."

Milad grumbles as he accelerates. En-Nahr Street means crossing crowded districts again, traveling roads encumbered with debris, risking all kinds of detours. He'd rather have headed straight for the highway bordering the coastline.

They arrive at the Nahr Beirut, the river marking the city limits. There, again, a barricade is slowing down traffic.

The militia take their time. Milad tells them, too, the story of the cousin in Juniyah.

Why not tell them the truth? Karim wonders all of a sudden. What's so awful about wanting to go to Chlifa? They'd let us by just the same.

But maybe Antoine Milad takes pleasure in concocting a story to add an element of mystery to their journey. And an atmosphere of danger.

"What bothers me," Milad told them the day before, "is that you're going to be hiking pretty well the whole time along the boundary between the Syrian and Christian sectors. I don't know how it works in the countryside. I don't know whether you can allow yourselves to be seen and identified. Your best bet is to take deserted side roads, not use any major roads, avoid villages and farms. Follow the course of the Nahr el-Kelb, and the base of the mountains; cut across fields. Nature will always be kinder than other human beings."

This was probably why Milad had invented the story about a cousin in Juniyah. To hide them from others. So they really could disappear into the wilderness.

Finally the militiamen let them pass, and the car crosses the Nahr Beirut. They're in a district Milad is unfamiliar with, and despite its closeness, it takes them quite awhile to reach the highway.

Once there, they make slightly better time. Karim is surprised to see so many buildings, so many houses crammed between the road and the mountains.

"It's ugly," Maha declares abruptly, her voice conveying a mixture of scorn and disappointment. "I thought we'd see the countryside once we were out of the city. Fields, flowers, orchards, trees gently climbing the mountain slopes. But there's nothing but concrete."

"When I was a boy," Milad answers, "the coastal road really was between the mountain and the sea. Then unregulated development started along the coast. It was a race to see who could build the most luxurious hotel, the biggest building. Developers launched an attack on the mountains . . . leading to the mess you see before you. Of course, the years of war and abandon haven't helped matters any."

"Yes, but the light," Karim murmurs, motioning to the huge expanse of sky that seems to spill over to the left. "The light . . . "

"Yes, there's still the light," agrees Milad. "As well as some worthwhile views," he adds just as the car penetrates a tunnel cut through the core of a rocky spur jutting into the sea. "Look."

As soon as they emerge from the tunnel, Milad turns off the highway and drives a hundred meters or so along a small road off to the right. Then he parks the car on the side and motions them to step out.

"The Nahr el-Kelb," he announces with pride, pointing to the water rushing at the bottom of a deep gorge. "In ancient times, they called it the Lycus. Does the name ring a bell?"

His young companions confess it doesn't, hoping the journalist won't launch into a lengthy historical explanation.

"Nahr el-Kelb," Maha repeats nevertheless. "The River of the Dog. Why did they give it that name?"

"It's said that a long time ago on this spot, a statue of a dog howled so loudly at the enemy's approach that the sound could be heard for leagues around. But certain scientific and pedestrian minds claim the howling was only the wind blowing through cracks in the rocky headland."

"And those shapes over there that look like monuments. What are they?" Karim asks.

"Commemorative stela. When I was a boy, not a year went by that we didn't come here on a school outing. My friends and I loved to run all over the place, tearing down the steep slopes to the water. . . . Unfortunately, our teachers didn't bring us here for the fun, but for the culture. This historic site—which is important for a host of reasons I'll spare you—has seventeen stela commemorating migrations, victories, events that occurred over a period of more than three thousand years. There are Egyptian and Assyrian stela, inscriptions in Latin, Greek, Arabic, French, English. The oldest stela dates back to Ramses II, to the thirteenth century BC, the most recent to the French troops' evacuation of Lebanon in 1946. . . ."

All those people, thinks Karim. All those people who've passed by here. Famous people and others like my father who left no stela, no trace of their passing. And now it's our turn. We're going to follow the Nahr el-Kelb and plunge into all that greenery along its narrow fault, high above the thin stream of water bearing the grandiose name "river."

THEY WALK TO A BRIDGE deep in the heart of the greenery, an old Arab bridge that forms a gracious arc above the Nahr el-Kelb. They've decided to have one last snack together before separating, before Milad returns to Beirut and they start on the long road to Chlifa.

After their snack, Milad hugs Karim close to him. He kisses Maha on the forehead.

"Good-bye, children. Godspeed."

Neither of them dreams of taking offense at his "children," not even Maha, who the night before rebelled at being called a little girl. Karim is strangely touched at leaving this man who, two days earlier, was only known to him by name. As for Maha, she clutches the postcard of the Lady with the Unicorn that Antoine Milad gave her.

"Until you find your dream, sweetheart," was all Milad said as he held it out to her. Maha's eyes filled with tears.

The two young people secure their knapsacks on their shoulders. Jad, wound in a big shawl, is firmly attached to Karim's chest.

"I'll watch you go," says Milad abruptly.

Maha and Karim cross the old bridge, then without looking back, turn right and follow the ridge overhanging the Nahr el-Kelb gorge. The vegetation is so thick that Antoine Milad soon loses sight of them.

"God protect you," he murmurs before he, too, leaves.

At first they walk at a brisk pace as though filled with a sense of urgency, straining toward the distant goal they've set themselves, as if to reach it as soon as possible.

The sun, already high in the sky, beats down on their young shoulders stretched taut under the knapsacks' straps.

The hikers penetrate a landscape that gradually opens ahead of them. They are enveloped in silence, assailed by strange scents. The scent of earth, water, flowers and trees. The scent of peace, Karim thinks as he breathes deeply. The chirping of a cricket suddenly pierces the silence, and Maha stops, thrilled.

"I think this is the first time I've ever heard a real cricket."

"Sure a nice break from the whistling of shrapnel."

"We've just barely left, and all that already seems so far away. . . ."

The terrain, a gradual but steady climb, is rough, strewn with stones, high grasses, hollows and mounds that make progress difficult. The heavily loaded knapsacks don't make the task any easier for Karim and Maha, who aren't used to so much exertion. After a while, they can feel pain in their calves, their thighs and their backs. Their breathing accelerates. They can feel their hearts beating right up in their temples, in the tips of their fingers.

"At this rate, we won't hold out very long," Maha suddenly says, breathless.

"Or else we'll be ready for the Olympics."

"How about we stop awhile?"

"If you really can't go any farther, we'll stop. But I kind of wanted to save our break for the Jeita cave. It shouldn't be much farther. It used to be a popular tourist spot."

"Now we're tourists, are we?" Maha teases.

"It's called combining business with pleasure," Karim replies in a no-nonsense voice.

Maha raises her eyes.

"Tourists it is!" she sighs.

A LITTLE LATER, sitting not far from the cave, both feet in the icy water of the Nahr el-Kelb, Maha admits that being a tourist has its good side.

"And its not-so-good side," she adds with a glance at the abandoned tourist facilities and the solid bars that block the entrance to the cave—or rather the caves, since there are two levels. The lower one is a passage to one of the Nahr el-Kelb's main river branches according to the tourist guide Antoine Milad gave them. "I was so looking forward to finally seeing some stalactites and stalagmites. Ever since I was little, that's been my dream. Do you think if we scouted around a bit, we might find a secret entrance?"

"No way!" replies Karim. "This cave can't have been visited for ages, and I hate to imagine what we might find inside. And I'm not just talking about holes in the ground or harmless bats or spiders."

What Karim doesn't say is that the very idea of going into a cave makes him shiver with distaste to the core of his being. He feels a definite revulsion at the thought of descending into the bowels of the earth, finding himself in a dark, enclosed, suffocating world.

"Haven't you had enough cellars and shelters?" he resumes, nearly belligerent. "Barely out of one hole, you want to scuttle down another?"

Maha looks at him, surprised by the fierceness of his reaction.

"It's not the same thing."

"It is so."

Maha doesn't answer right away. She takes her feet out of the water, puts her socks back on, her shoes. Then she starts preparing Jad's bottle. The burner has to be turned on, the water boiled, the powder added to the water once it cools down. When everything's ready, she settles back to give her brother his bottle.

"Well, then, since we're not going on a real tour of the caves, we can visit them in our minds," she decides. "Read out loud what the guidebook says."

Shrugging his shoulders, Karim complies with what he sees as her whim.

"One of Lebanon's top-ranking tourist sites as shown by the number of its visitors," he begins, *"the Jeita cave richly deserves its renown.* Great," he grumbles with an air of disgust, "there they go talking about 'before' again."

"Go on," orders Maha, who has closed her eyes.

"To its considerable size—not in itself a unique feature—the cave adds an extraordinary wealth of concretions which unquestionably rank it among the most beautiful in the world."

"What are concretions?"

"I don't know. Probably your stalactites and stalagmites."

"Wow!" Maha sighs happily. "Go on, go on."

So Karim keeps reading. He describes the caves' general aspect, gives the background on the discovery and exploration of the site, lists visiting hours and facilities. Maha loves the last paragraph. She repeats some of the expressions that studded the text: *crystallizations, excavations, concretions,* that word again. One sentence in particular seems to tickle her fancy: *For thousands and thousands of years, billions and billions of droplets have left minute deposits of calcite that slowly join to form concretions whose diversity, as much as their appearance, gives rise to flights of the imagination.*

"Can you believe it?" she whispers. "Thousands and thousands of years, billions and billions of droplets. Right beside us. All to create the 'concretions' just over there behind those few bars. It almost makes you dizzy. All right, close your eyes now and follow me. We're heading into the upper cave. The ground is reddish-brown. Suddenly, in the flashlight's beam, strange, unreal shapes appear. Shapes like arms, disembodied arms pointing every which way."

"Don't you think you're getting kind of morbid?"

But Maha ignores the interruption and continues describing the scenery inside the cave as she imagines it. Cathedral spires, petrified algae, twisted needles, gnomes and fantastic animal shapes frozen in lime-stone. Concretions that exist for them alone.

Her words lull them. Jad dozes with his bottle in his mouth, a drop of milk on the corner of his lips. Karim and Maha decide to lie down for a bit of a rest. All three fall asleep under the shade of a round-headed pine.

WHEN THEY WAKE UP, the sun is already low in the sky. The trees' shadows lengthen on the ground. Far away, above the city, a rocket has just exploded.

"At this rate, it's going to take us a month to get to Chlifa," Maha remarks.

"We can still walk for a few more hours today," replies Karim. "As long as it doesn't get too dark."

They continue to make their way in the golden light of day's end. They follow what they assume to be a secondary branch of the Nahr el-Kelb. The stream is tiny, but it has dug a deep, steep ravine. Actually, the two hikers have doubts about whether there's even any water left at the bottom of this narrow fault whose sinuous path they follow. They make slow but steady progress. The terrain starts to climb sharply now, and sometimes they have to stop to try to catch their breath. They take advantage of these breaks to look around them. They take turns carrying Jad. Even though the baby isn't heavy, his weight, added to the weight of the knapsacks and the fatigue from the climb, ends up seeming like an enormous burden.

At nightfall, they stop, pitch the small tent and have a quick bite to eat. Maha looks after her brother as though in her sleep. Jad gurgles, kicking his chubby legs, his little arms trying to grab Maha's braids.

When it's time for bed, Maha brings out her postcard of the Lady with the Unicorn and studies it for a long time by the light from the flashlight.

"This unicorn is so beautiful but so sad. Why do you think it's so sad?"

"How should I know?" answers Karim, who can think only of sleep. "Besides, what makes you think it's sad? Maybe it just has heartburn."

"No, these aren't the eyes of a unicorn with an aching stomach. These are the eyes of a unicorn with an aching soul."

"A unicorn's soul! Are you sure the Prophet mentioned unicorns having a soul?"

Maha doesn't answer. She blows a soft kiss in the direction of the picture, turns off the flashlight and murmurs before falling into a deep sleep, "In any case, I for one will protect this unicorn until my dying day."

Karim sighs in the dark. There's no doubt about it, this girl has some strange ideas.

But soon Karim, too, sinks into a deep, dreamless sleep. He forgets Maha and her strange ideas. He forgets menace and danger. He forgets the war rumbling in the distance. He sleeps.

"Ouch!" grimaces Maha as she wakes up the next morning. "So this is what it's like to be sore all over."

As soon as she steps outside the tent, however, she discovers a landscape of breathtaking beauty . . . and promptly forgets being sore. From where she stands, she can see the whole Nahr el-Kelb valley that drops gently to the sea, shimmering with light under a vast blue sky. She discovers hills, woods, villages nestled in small glens or perched on rocky peeks, steeples thrusting upward to the sky.

"Karim, come see."

Karim crawls out, his hair disheveled, still looking half asleep.

"Oh!"

He, too, feels the impact of the landscape. The day before, in the dark, they hadn't seen much of anything despite the rising moon. And they were so exhausted that they could think of only one thing—sleep.

Their contemplation is interrupted by furious cries from Jad, who doesn't appreciate being abandoned and is demanding his bottle with great conviction.

"Babies never stop drinking, do they?" exclaims Karim, thinking of how much space Jad takes up despite his small size. And what a set of lungs!

"If only that were all they did," sighs Maha. "Babies never stop shitting either."

"Maha!" cries Karim, shocked by her choice of words. "Nada would never have used that word."

"No, she wouldn't, would she?" retorts Maha, stung. "But she wouldn't have been the one to change his diaper either!"

And with angry steps, she heads toward the tent.

She changes the baby in silence and puts him in Karim's arms. Then she empties the last of the water from the gourd into the small pan.

"Heat the water up for the bottle. I'm going down to the river to rinse out this diaper and the one from last night that I left in a plastic bag. I'll fill the gourd up, too."

As she begins descending the steep slope, Karim calls out, "A word of advice. Fill the gourd first."

"What do you take me for, a bloody idiot? Of course I'll fill the gourd first."

She walks a few steps farther, then adds, "And don't bother telling me Nada would never have said 'bloody idiot.' I know."

Karim watches her disappear.

"Kid," he says to Jad, who's still yelling for his bottle, "your sister's going to drive me crazy one of these days. All the same, I hope she doesn't break her neck in the ravine."

MAHA DIDN'T BREAK HER NECK in the ravine, although she did slip several times, each time starting an avalanche of pebbles that raced down the slope before falling into the water with little *plops* that she found reassuring. At least there was water at the bottom.

She filled the gourd and rinsed the diapers (in that order) then climbed back up, grabbing onto any hold she could find.

"Oof!" she sighs as she sinks down beside Karim, who's giving Jad his bottle as best he can. "That's one way of working up an appetite. I'm starving."

"Madam, breakfast is served," replies Karim, motioning with his chin toward two thick slabs of bread and jam sitting on a hanky.

Maha raises her eyebrows in surprise.

"You had time to get the milk ready and make bread and jam? Nada was right—you really are perfect."

And she pounces on the bread, which she devours, almost without taking a breath.

Karim, his interest piqued, goes over and over the

few words she's just spoken. Nada said he was perfect? What did she mean? And what else did she say? How much does Maha know about him?

ALL DAY, THESE QUESTIONS HOUND HIM. He walks, he climbs, he carries Jad, he's aware of a pain between his shoulders, of the effort it takes to move one leg, then the other, again and again. But always, like an obsessive litany, the questions return. Sterile, useless, no doubt selfish questions that hammer at his head and his heart. What did Nada think of me? What did she say about me? Did she love me? And who was she really? Nada. A name. A smile. A scent tinged with sweetness. The fleeting curve of a breast. A too-quick kiss. And now this ache that digs at his insides.

At one point, they come to a road, which they cross after making sure it's deserted. From time to time, they glimpse a farm in the distance, sometimes even shapes walking or working in the fields, but they encounter no one.

The heat is so intense at noon that they decide to stop for a few hours in the shade of some trees. After, they'll continue on into the evening like the day before.

In the afternoon, the bombing starts up again in the distance, but they hardly notice. Over there are bombs; here are trees, rocks, birds and butterflies. The two worlds have nothing in common. Maybe this is how one forgets atrocities. By distancing oneself. By acting as if they don't exist.

THEY WATCH THE SUN SINK into the sea, far away on the horizon.

"Watching something like this," Karim says suddenly, "makes me feel much more like praying than any muezzin's[1] call to prayers."

---

[1]muezzin: Muslim religious crier who calls the faithful to prayer five times a day from the minaret of a mosque

"You're not facing the right direction," Maha points out. "Mecca would be behind us. Or at least, I think it would be."

Karim doesn't respond right away. When he does it's to ask, "What about you? Do you pray five times a day, prostrating yourself in the direction of Mecca?"

"Five times, no. That's a lot, don't you think?"

"But it's one of the five pillars of Islam, one of the five obligations of individuals in our religion. Are you a bad Muslim?"

"That's what my mother, Mrs. Farhat and even Nada used to say. But I don't think I'm a bad Muslim. A bit care-less maybe, but not bad. Besides, I'm still a 'little girl' as you keep reminding me, and so I don't have to meet all the obligations yet. Anyway, I do pray regularly, I fast during Ramadan, and I believe, like it says in the *chahâda*[2] "that the only god is God and that Mohammed is His prophet." As for giving alms and the pilgrimage to Mecca, I'll worry about those when I'm grown up. So you see I'm not such a bad Muslim. What about you? Are you a good Muslim?"

Karim thinks it over for a minute.

"Probably not. Actually, my mother is Christian, and my father quit going to the mosque a long time ago. So maybe our home wasn't the best environment for religious fervor. I believe in God, yes. In the God of Moses, Jesus and Mohammed. But I don't think about it much. I sometimes read the Koran. Some of the sourates[3] are quite beautiful."

As he's speaking, Karim can't get over the fact that he's talking about religion like this with Maha. He also can't get over how attentive she is. Sometimes he has a hard time remembering she's only twelve.

THEY START WALKING AGAIN toward the mountains that tower in the distance, forming a seemingly impassable

---

[2]*chahâda:* Islam profession of faith, affirming God's oneness
[3]sourates: chapters of the Koran

barrier. If Antoine Milad hadn't given them a detailed map of the region, if he hadn't assured them that a path to the other side of the mountain did exist, they would have thought twice about continuing toward that distant wall of snow-topped peaks, which seems to recede as they advance.

"This is incredible!" exclaims Maha during one of their numerous breaks. "No matter how much we walk, the mountains are still as far away. Do you think maybe they're bewitched?"

Karim wonders pretty much the same thing but won't let himself get discouraged. He answers with somewhat forced optimism, "Of course not. We're making good progress. Look at that big cypress tree over there. It's getting bigger by the minute. If the mountains still don't seem any closer, it's because the humidity clouds the air and distorts distances. . . ."

"Hurrah for science!" Maha retorts in a mocking tone. "Are you really sure about that?"

"Well . . . "

"Just as I thought. A bit more conviction there, professor!"

AFTER SUNSET, THEY NEAR ANOTHER ROAD, a larger one dotted with villages at intervals too close for comfort. One thought is uppermost in their minds—crossing the road as quickly and discreetly as possible. For discretion's sake, they decide to wait until nightfall. Two shadows walking among the shadows shouldn't attract too much attention. They settle comfortably into a wooded hollow and wait for twilight.

"Let's go," Karim declares after a while. "It must be dark enough now. Besides, if we wait too long, the moon will give us away."

They stand up and, after a careful look around, cross

the road and head into the fields on the other side. They walk fast to get away from the villages as quickly as possible.

"If we're where we should be," Karim had said while they waited, "according to the map, the village on our left is Mazraat Kfardibiane and the one on our right is Bqaatouta. Or maybe Boqaatet Kanaâne."

Right now Maha couldn't care less which villages they are. All she wants is to see the last of them.

"We'll walk for a little while longer," suggests Karim, "then settle down for the night. Despite your pessimism, young lady, we aren't all that far from the mountains. By stretching your arm out, you could touch them . . . almost. Tomorrow, we can veer more to the north to meet up with the path we were told about by—"

He stops, struck dumb at the scene awaiting them on the other side of a stand of trees.

The moon has just risen, lighting up a landscape bristling with white, jagged rocks. In the distance, the foot of the mountains is ringed with thousands of low, terraced walls.

"Moonstones," Maha murmurs.

They both try to find, in any language, the words to best describe this unreal and haunting spot.

"It's otherworldly," Maha finally says. "A ghostly moonscape."

Silently, they move forward into the lunar landscape, among the rocks thrusting skyward, seemingly drawn by the pull of the moon. The rocks stretch for kilometers.

"There are your stalagmites," Karim says.

"If you want to put it that way. But stalagmites grow deep underground, and these stone needles have fallen from the moon. They're orphans of the moon reaching out to her with all their strength. But the moon is icy in her indifference. She simply bathes them in her white light. She stays there, luring them, taunting them, but never taking them back."

"Enough already," interrupts Karim, who doesn't like this story of orphans and futile efforts.

And then, walking among the rocks, they discover the ruins. Ruins from long ago.

There are columns, something that must have been a temple, two square towers.

"Roman ruins," murmurs Karim in a dreamy tone. "Do you realize there were people here a long time ago? They prayed here, maybe even lived here. It's beautiful, isn't it? So peaceful."

"Uh-huh. But don't you think it's strange how beautiful old ruins are and how horrible young ruins are, like the ones in Beirut? Do you think that hundreds or thousands of years from now, people will feel inspired walking through the ruins of Beirut, saying how beautiful, peaceful and romantic they are?"

"You and your ideas!" retorts Karim, who's troubled in spite of himself. Beirut's ruins romantic and peaceful? No way. This is what he tries to explain to Maha. "But . . . no, it won't be peaceful or romantic. There've been too many deaths, too much blood, too many screams."

"What about these ruins and all the other ruins in the world? Weren't there deaths, blood, screams? In Troy, in Rome, in . . . in . . . I don't know, Babylon or Sparta or Baalbek? Weren't there wars, battles, atrocities? But now all we see is the peaceful, romantic side. Don't you find that revolting, all those forgotten dead?"

Karim doesn't say anything. There's nothing to say. A lifetime wouldn't be enough to try to understand.

"THIS WOULD BE A PERFECT SPOT for a fire," Maha sighs a bit later on. "A huge bonfire."

"A huge bonfire that would as good as tell the whole world where we are," retorts Karim. Instead, he lights the burner that Milad gave them. "So, minestrone, a can of tuna and dates, Mademoiselle?"

Maha sighs. Of course, minestrone, tuna and dates. As usual. When Antoine Milad filled their knapsacks with provisions, he gave a small smile as he pointed at the cans of tuna, pouches of dehydrated minestrone and the huge package of dates.

"Not much variety, but there's lots of it. You won't die of starvation with this."

"Starvation, no; monotony, yes."

"A bit of monotony never killed anyone."

Every evening, every meal the same. Tuna, minestrone and dates. Instant coffee. Milk for Jad, a small jar of baby food. "I can't wait till he's finished all the baby food," Karim grumbled the first time he lifted up his knapsack. "These little jars weigh a ton."

"Not as much as the tuna," retorted Maha, who'd been saddled with the cans.

After the meal, Karim rinses the dishes while Maha changes Jad's diaper, washes the dirty diaper and sings a sad little song—always the same one—to her brother to put him to sleep. Karim can't quite catch the words, but he doesn't dare ask her to sing any louder.

They set up camp in the middle of the ruins, in the mineral moonscape glowing strangely in the moonlight.

Before going into the tent to sleep, Karim and Maha linger outside to watch the night sky studded with pale stars they can barely see in the moonlight.

"I love the night," Maha says in a soft voice.

And the next minute—"I hate the night," she announces just as softly.

Karim raises his eyebrows.

"Make up your mind, will you. Is it love or is it hate?"

"Well . . . both," Maha answers as though stating the obvious. "It's the same for everything." She stops for a second and looks as though she's trying to find a way to make him understand. "Do you sometimes read interviews with movie stars or sports heroes?" Karim shakes his head. "Well, I do, all the time. I love them. You know, the kind of interview where people are asked what their favorite season is or their favorite food or their favorite color. It's not their answers I'm interested in. It's that they *always* have an answer. That they can say, 'My favorite color is red,' or 'My favorite season is summer.' Me, my favorite color's red. And green. And yellow. And white. When I say one thing, I often feel like I could say the opposite and it would be just as true. Yes, I love the night when I can tell myself stories in the dark alone in my own bed. Or when everything's so quiet, so immense, like tonight. I hate the night when bombs are going off all over. When people take advantage of the shadows to kill, rape, loot. So you see, everything's true."

"Or everything's false," Karim remarks.

"If you want to put it that way."

"Is that why old Mrs. Farhat called you a liar?"

"No, what I just told you is the kind of thing she doesn't understand, the kind of thing she wouldn't understand even if you explained it to her for a hundred years. No, she was talking about something else. About the times I say I'm going over to my friend Hiba's to study when I really sneak out for a smoke behind the building, just under her windows. I hate smoking, but I love to shock that old bag. Or when I come home earlier than usual saying the teacher was sick and let us go when really I just skipped so I wouldn't have to take a math test."

"What's the point of telling all those lies?"

"To get me in trouble usually," Maha answers with a little laugh. "What about you? Don't you ever lie?"

Taken unaware, Karim hesitates before answering.

"No. Well, yes, probably a little, like everyone else. But not . . . not for the same reasons. I hate lying."

"Oh, that's right, 'the perfect young man' as Nada said."

Those words again! This time, under cover of darkness, Karim decides to ask the question that's been haunting him all day.

"Nada told you about me?"

"You know, Nada and I didn't talk that much."

"But that's the second time you've said Nada called me a perfect young man. And the other night when we left the shelter, you knew we'd kissed. So Nada must have told you."

Maha doesn't answer right away. She looks lost in thought as she winds one end of her long braid around her finger. Finally, she makes up her mind. Staring straight into Karim's eyes, she raises her chin with a look Karim's beginning to recognize and announces with a touch of defiance, "No, she didn't tell me. I read it in her diary. She kept it hidden under her mattress, which, if you ask me, wasn't very bright. *Everybody* knows that's the first place anyone would look. She could have shown a bit more imagination. Tacked it up behind a drawer or hid it on the bookshelves. But Nada never had any imagination."

"Liar, snoop. . . . You know I'm beginning to wonder whether Mrs. Farhat wasn't right."

"Well," Maha cries out angrily, "I'm beginning to believe my sister was right—you really are a perfect young man. You'd make a good policeman or how about a judge. Stern, pompous, quick to condemn. I hate perfect people. And for once, the opposite isn't true."

With these words, Maha disappears into the tent. Karim hears her jerk the zipper up on her sleeping bag.

Karim gazes at the landscape in front of him without seeing it. The conversation with Maha has troubled him. It's the first time he's met someone who can get to him the way she does. Maha is naive and fierce, fragile and tough at the same time. He never knows if she's going to start laughing and skipping or clench her fists and hurl her rage in his face.

And her accusations make him uncomfortable. Is he really the rigid, stern person she's described? A perfect young man? What can that mean to her? Intuitively, Karim knows the words don't mean the same thing to Maha that they might have meant to Nada. And he still doesn't know what Nada meant by them. In fact, does he want to be perfect? Maybe, deep down. Is that such a bad thing? In any case, he knows very well he isn't perfect. He's too touchy, selfish, proud. . . . Maybe not always, but . . .

Suddenly, he realizes that Maha is right. It isn't easy to say a thing is true, unchanging, definitive.

"I don't understand her," he murmurs to the night. "She's cheeky, full of flaws, but she's also got guts and smarts . . . and something mysterious. Something like an awareness that doesn't fit with her frail body and her clear voice. And now she's angry with me. Tomorrow we'll have to make up. It would be stupid to keep traveling together without speaking to each other."

It's Karim's turn to slip into the tent, but he has trouble getting to sleep. His thoughts whirl around in his head without his being able to follow any one thought logically and clearly. Just as he drifts off, he wonders which of his flaws could win Maha over, make her less tough on him.

The next morning, Karim is awakened by Jad's cries.

It's light outside, the baby's lying beside him in the tent and there's no sign of Maha.

"She can't have just disappeared, leaving me her brother," grumbles Karim, still half asleep. "Of course not. Not after what she said the other night." Karim can still see her fervent face lifted to his, hear her clear voice saying Jad is all she has. "No, she hasn't gone and left him. But where can she be?"

As though in answer to his question, sounds can be heard close by. Karim hears crackling, rustling and Maha's slightly breathless voice.

"Come on, that's it, that's a good girl. There, that's it. Whoa . . . stop pulling. I'm not going to hurt you. There, my black beauty, there you go."

Intrigued, Karim pokes his head out of the tent. Has Maha found a cat or maybe a hen?

Well no, the creature Maha is trying to coax isn't a cat or a hen. It's a goat, a black, long-haired goat that's gazing at Maha with inscrutable eyes.

"She's hardheaded, this one," mutters Maha.

Maha has twisted one of Jad's diapers into a makeshift loop that she now tries to put around the goat's neck. She's also holding a length of rope. Who knows where that came from. She's obviously trying to leash the goat like a little dog.

"She does look stubborn," Karim agrees from where he's still kneeling in the tent opening. "If you take into account her big eyes, her pointed chin and her black, tangled hair, she's the spitting image of you. We could call her little Maha."

"Very funny," retorts Maha without bothering to look his way. "I only hope there's less hair on my chin . . . which isn't as pointed as all that, thank-you very much. But instead of insulting me, you should be helping me

tie up this damn creature. Yes, my pretty one, yes, sweetheart," she continues as she tries to pat the black forehead. "Yes, you're coming with us. You'll see, we're going
on a wonderful trip. What's more, we'll be able to help
you with your load. Don't you think her udder looks
swollen?"

"You know, goats, well, I . . ." Karim begins cautiously.

"At last, something you know nothing about!" Maha
exclaims delighted. "Maybe he isn't as perfect as he
looks after all," she says to the goat, which is still resisting her. "Maybe we'll be able to make something of him
yet."

"Are you sure it's really called an udder for goats?"

"It was too good to last," sighs Maha. "What do you
want me to call it?" she asks, motioning to the teats.
"Breasts?"

"Well, you're sure no example of the legendary modesty of Arab women," Karim remarks as he extricates
himself from the tent.

But his voice isn't rigid or stern this time, and Maha
doesn't take offense at his remark.

Karim walks toward Maha and her goat while in the
tent, Jad howls with renewed vigor.

"Actually, the . . . things do look swollen," he admits
as he scratches his head, looking perplexed.

"Well, then, let's milk her," Maha decides. "If only I
could . . . There!" she cries joyfully. "Finally, I got the
halter around her neck. There, there, pretty one; there,
there, my black beauty. You're going to stand quietly
now while this big oaf milks you. Yes, you are. . . ."

"Me!" Karim chokes. "But I don't know how."

"We figured that out on our own. What about me? Do
you think I've spent my life milking goats on the corner
of Mazraa Street and Borj Abi Haïdar? I don't see how it
can be all that complicated. You grab the teats and pull."

Resigned, Karim goes for the pan, sets it under the goat in the spot where, in all probability, the milk will flow, then crouches down beside the animal. The operation has a vaguely sexual side that makes him uncomfortable. Probably because I have a dirty mind, he thinks, not that the explanation makes the job any easier.

He finally decides to grab onto the teats and exert a bit of pressure.

"Harder," Maha says impatiently. "You don't have to caress her, just milk her."

Karim can feel himself blush a deep red, he's not sure whether from anger or shame.

He squeezes harder and pulls down slightly.

"Slide your hands up and down," Maha suggests.

He slides his hands up and down. Finally, a few drops spurt out . . . and fall everywhere but in the pan. Karim expects some smart remark from Maha, but surprisingly, she doesn't say a thing.

Karim finally finds a way of making the milk squirt. He probably wouldn't win the national goat-milking contest, but the level of milk is gradually rising in the pan.

"I think that's it," he declares at last when the teats seem empty and limp under his fingers.

"Take the pan away, quick before she kicks it," Maha suggests quietly.

She's abandoned the mocking, haughty tone that bothered Karim so much.

Karim picks the pan up and gets to his feet. Only then does he realize that he's drenched in sweat and as exhausted as though he's run a long race.

"Boy—a goatherd's life is sure no picnic."

Suddenly, Maha bursts out laughing. A clear, fresh laugh like a spring bubbling up from under the moss.

It's the first time Karim has heard her laugh like this, freely, without mockery, and he is captivated by the laughter that flows into the early morning.

The two of them laugh among the ruins in the middle of the moonstones glowing pink in the rising sun, between the bleating goat and Jad howling himself hoarse deep inside the tent. They laugh until tears come to their eyes, until their stomachs ache, until they topple over. Sometimes, they almost seem ready to calm down. Then one look at each other and they start laughing all over again.

"We're laughing un-con-trol-la-bly," hiccups Karim.

"Con . . . what?" Maha chokes out.

"Not con, *un*con. Uncon . . . uncon . . . Oh, I can't take anymore," Karim gasps.

It's been a long time since he's been this happy. So idiotically happy.

("Baa!" says the goat.)

ONCE THEY CALM DOWN—even uncontrollable laughter has to come to an end sometime—they tie the goat to a tree, share the still-warm milk (Maha maintains that Jad is too little for this kind of milk, and Karim doesn't argue, especially since he himself thinks it tastes very strange), then Karim goes to get Jad while Maha works away at the burner.

"Ohhh, is this kid filthy!" Karim exclaims on his way out of the tent, holding Jad at arm's length.

"Please, don't make me laugh," implores Maha. "I hurt all over."

"Well, then, repeat after me: Karim is an imperfect young man full of flaws."

"Karim is a flaw full of imperfect young man."

"It lacks conviction, but I'll let it pass. Here, I have the perfect remedy for uncontrollable laughter."

And he sets Jad in her arms, Jad who right now is a howling, stinking, pee-drenched package.

THEY SAID FAREWELL to their moonscape and their ruins. According to the guidebook, the name of the site is Qalat Fakra. A little farther along, they should find a stream topped by a natural bridge of impressive beauty. Maha and Karim have nothing against beauty, but they are more attracted by the idea of freshening up a bit in the stream.

They find the stream, dutifully admire the perfectly symmetrical arch that tops it and thankfully dunk their feet (and several other parts of their anatomy) in the rushing, icy water. Big, round rocks seem to have been positioned just right in the streambed, so they can cross without danger. Once across, they continue on their route, which now takes them steadily up.

Before leaving Qalat Fakra, they had pored over the map of the region, unsure of which way to go. They know where they want to end up, no doubt about that. Next to Akura, a bit farther north, where the ancient Roman road starts that will take them to the other side of Mount Lebanon, a few kilometers from Chlifa. But they weren't sure what the best route would be. According to the map, one route follows the base of the mountains in one long curve before reaching Akura. Unfortunately, this route also passes through several villages, and the young travelers had wondered about the advisability of venturing into inhabited areas. So they decided to take the mountain route.

"Like Antoine Milad said, 'Nature will always be kinder than human beings,' or something along those lines," Karim remembered.

"So we continue our wild, adventurous life," Maha rejoiced. "And now that we have Black Beard, even if we get lost, we won't die of hunger. Isn't that right, my pretty?" she added in the goat's direction.

Black Beard gave a condescending nod of her bearded chin.

"We won't get lost," Karim said with conviction. "We just have to climb to a sort of plateau and then turn north. We'll be in a valley then. By following the valley, we should end up next to Aphaca, not too far from Akura, *inch Allah.*"

Now, several hours later, they have to retrace their steps for the second time because the slope they're on is cut off by a steep precipice, and there's no way they can continue that way with a goat and a baby. With the goat, maybe. But the baby . . .

So they retrace their steps and try their luck elsewhere, at a spot where the mountain rises steeply. Their progress is slow and difficult. Black Beard stops in the most awkward places, and they still haven't found their "sort of plateau."

Obviously, Karim says to himself, it's the kind of thing that seems a lot clearer on a map than on tree-covered, extremely uneven terrain. Things seem more confusing when you're face to face with them.

They aren't afraid of getting lost, not yet, but they're starting to wonder if they shouldn't have followed the road, even if it meant walking all night and sleeping during the day in the bottom of a ditch or in the bushes.

"Uh-uh, not so," Maha concludes. "We just can't be in such a hurry, that's all."

They interrupt their journey with frequent stops. Maha takes advantage of the breaks to try to identify the trees and plants they encounter.

"That's a pine tree, I'm sure, and that one's an oak. But what about this funny-looking plant?"

Karim has to confess his ignorance of anything botanical.

"For once your perfection would have been of some use," sighs Maha. "Too bad. We'll die ignorant."

Finally, after many steps and many stops, they discover their plateau shortly before nightfall. A valley opens to the north, between a hill on the left and a taller mountain on the right. They begin traveling up the valley, but soon it's so dark they can't even see where they're walking. They have to resign themselves to spending the night surrounded by mountains.

After sunset, a brisk wind began to blow that's now making them shiver. They set the tent up quickly and seek shelter inside, glad for the warmth created by their three bodies squeezed into the confined space. Jad is lying between them, and, as he does every night, Karim hopes they won't crush him.

Outside, Black Beard pulls on her rope and bleats plaintively.

"Do you think there are wolves in the mountains?" Maha suddenly asks. "We wouldn't want anything to happen to Black Beard. You know, like in the story 'The Brave Little Goat.' She fought all through the night, only to have the wolf eat her come morning."

"I'm sure there aren't any wolves around here," Karim replies, trying to sound reassuring. "Anyway, what do you want us to do? Bring her inside the tent with us? With her goatee tickling our noses? And think how fatal one whiff of her breath would be."

Maha gives a little laugh.

"Come on, don't worry about your goat," Karim continues. "Sweet dreams."

"You, too," Maha replies playfully. "Dreams of me."

And, after one last look at the Lady with the Unicorn, she turns off the flashlight.

In the dark, Karim grabs onto a long braid and pulls gently.

"You sure don't let modesty cramp your style," he says half whispering.

"Nothing cramps my style," she points out.

And she falls asleep, a big smile on her lips.

"She's getting used to us, don't you think? You'd almost say she's smiling. And she's much better about walking now. . . ."

Karim bursts out laughing.

"Here we have Mademoiselle Maha, world specialist on goats and goat smiles. Where there isn't a unicorn . . . "

"Of course, she doesn't have a unicorn's class," Maha admits. "Anyway, I would never have tied up a unicorn. Unicorns are fragile. They're proud. They have to be free. You can't tie them up like lowly goats (sorry, Black Beard). You admire them from afar, once, if you're really lucky, and then live with that memory for the rest of your life."

Karim, who can't tell if she really believes in unicorns or not, thinks it best to keep quiet. His companion is feeling upbeat, and he has no desire to see that change.

All around, it's an upbeat kind of day. The weather's wonderful, the goat let herself be milked without a complaint, Jad is gurgling more than he's crying and they're making better time than the day before in this harsh, bracing landscape. Even the minestrone and tuna seem to taste different.

The valley stretches out farther than they'd expected, but the hike is an easy one. Once again, Karim is struck by the scents rising from the earth, from the thickets, from the proliferation of plant life that surrounds them.

"If we crossed the mountains here, do you think we'd be in Chlifa?" Maha asks halfway through the afternoon, motioning to the summits looming to their right.

"Maybe. The problem is we can't just cross anywhere. Did you see the snow? We have to find a pass we can get through, and the Roman road Milad told us about is certainly safer and more passable than any path we could open ourselves."

Maha stops and looks at the snow-covered peaks.

"I've never felt snow. Have you?"

Karim shakes his head, indicating he hasn't either.

"I always dreamed of lying down in the snow and waving my arms to make angel's wings," Maha confides. "I saw it in a movie once, and I promised myself that one day I'd make an angel."

They start up again and head toward the light-filled gap straight ahead where the valley seems to end.

"WELL, MY OLD FRIEND, some route this turned out to be," Maha remarks with friendly irony. "So that's Aphaca?"

They're standing on the brink of a drop, on the edge of a cliff that falls vertically from a dizzying height. The ground at the bottom seems incredibly far away. From the side of the cliff, somewhere below them, flows a spring that feeds the Nahr Ibrahim, the river of Adonis.

"You've got to admit the view's spectacular," retorts Karim. "Look at the torrent rushing to the cliff bottom, the valley making its way to the sea, the villages clinging here and there to the rocky peaks, all the lush vegetation shining in the rays of the setting sun."

"You should go into advertising. You've got real talent," remarks Maha, even as she, too, admires the panorama spread at their feet. "What do you think those red flowers are?"

Both the shores of the Nahr Ibrahim and the neighboring fields are strewn with red flowers.

"No idea," replies Karim, who has almost had it with Maha's botanical questions. "Red flowers. Personally, I'm more concerned about how we're going to get down from here."

"There's a path below us," announces Maha, who's leaning dangerously over the drop. "If we could get to it . . ."

But Karim's already pulling her back.

"Are you crazy or something? A little farther and you'd be making a crash landing a hundred meters down."

Maha shrugs her shoulders.

"Don't worry about me. I'm surefooted."

"Look after Jad and Black Beard instead while I do some exploring."

"Why do we have to go down anyway? A little farther on, we're just going to want to climb back up again. If we follow the cliff edge, we'll end up at Akura where the Roman road starts. And since the Roman road climbs the mountain, we're bound to come across it."

Karim takes out the map and examines it closely.

"You're right," he finally admits. "We can try following the cliff edge. But I'm afraid it might not always be possible. Our route could be cut off as soon as we come across a mountain stream."

"We'll see. In the meantime, I'm starting to get hungry."

After the meal, while Jad is gulping down his milk and Black Beard is grazing quietly on the long grass, Karim pulls out their guidebook from his knapsack and flips through it briefly.

"Anemones," he says suddenly.

Maha sends him a questioning look.

"Your red flowers, they've got to be anemones. Listen to this: *Born of an incestuous love affair between Cinyras, King of Cyprus, and his daughter Myrrha, Adonis was so extraordinarily beautiful that Aphrodite fell in love with him. One day while he was hunting in the forests of Lebanon, a wild boar sent by a jealous Mars (perhaps the wild boar was even Mars himself) charged and mortally wounded him. Learning of the accident, the goddess set out to find him, shedding tears as she ran through the mountains. She found her lover, cared for him but could not wrest him from a too-human death. Under the shade of Aphaca, where they had loved each other for the first time, Adonis and Aphrodite exchanged one last kiss. From the young god's blood spilled across the prairie, anemones sprang. . . .* It's obvious. The red flowers scattered along the banks are the blood of Adonis," he concludes, gesturing grandly toward the river winding below.

Maha's eyes are shining.

"Just think, gods made love here. Here. It's fabulous, it's fantastic, it's amazing, it's . . . "

"What amazes me is the wild boars. What if we come face to face with one?"

"Are you sure you call it a face when it's a wild boar?" asks Maha, delighted at the opportunity to get her own back.

Karim's only response is to rush her, making hideous snorting sounds, and grab Jad who, luckily, has just finished drinking.

"A monster!" cries Maha. "A monster just kidnapped my baby! Please, I beg you, monster, leave me my goat."

"Groink, groink!"

"Leave me my packages of minestrone, my cans of tuna and my dates . . . for pity's sake, monster, not my tuna!"

"Groink, groink!"

"On the other hand, if you could take my sinister young companion. I would be most grateful."

"GROINK!"

The monster sets Jad on the ground, throws himself on Maha and pretends to eat her.

"Groink, not bad, that little aftertaste of tuna. Yup, it makes up for all the rest, groink."

The monster, having eaten his fill, drops down beside Maha amid her peals of laughter.

"IF WE SPEND THE NIGHT where the Roman road starts," estimates Karim, "we have a chance of reaching Chlifa by the end of the day tomorrow."

They hurry along the cliff hoping to reach the Roman road before nightfall.

"As you so rightly pointed out," continues Karim, "we can't miss it since it follows the bottom of a valley that crosses our path. I just hope the way down won't be as steep as the cliff above the Aphaca cave."

So they hurry onward but tire quickly. All that climbing up and down, watching out for holes, thorns, rocks, carrying Jad, pulling Black Beard. However, they keep going because evening's approaching, it will soon be dark and they've made up their minds to camp close to the Roman road.

"It shouldn't be much farther now," mutters Karim just as he trips over a huge root. Since he's the one carrying Jad, he throws his hands forward to protect the baby as he falls. The upshot is two scraped hands and a baby, unhurt but awake and screaming. It's been time for his bottle for quite a while, but the two travelers haven't wanted to stop because it would slow their progress. As long as he isn't crying . . . they'd kept thinking.

"All right, all right, all right, we'll get your bottle ready."

With the remaining water, Maha prepares some milk, and Karim cleans his scraped hands. Nothing fatal, obviously, but still it hurts. Where on earth could that valley be? Could they have missed it? Impossible, you can't miss such a distinct valley. They can't have been going around in circles. They didn't leave the cliff's edge. What then?

They start up again as soon as Jad has been fed and changed. Karim goes first, flashlight in hand, and Maha follows. She's carrying Jad, pulling Black Beard and hoping against hope that the valley will soon appear.

"I don't like how the beam of light advertises our whereabouts," Karim says suddenly, his brow knit. "Who knows who's watching."

"Turn the light off, and let's stop here to sleep," Maha suggests.

"No. Not before we've reached the valley," Karim insists.

They keep walking, one step after another after another. "Three hundred and eight, three hundred and nine, three hundred and ten . . . " Maha counts to herself. "No, one thousand three hundred and ten. Uh-uh. Oh, who cares."

Finally, in the beam of the flashlight, Karim sees the terrain suddenly drop off.

"It's the valley, Maha! The valley!" he whispers excitedly. He doesn't dare speak any louder. He doesn't know how far away the Christian village of Akura is, and there's no way he wants anyone to hear them.

The slope is steep but manageable. Sometimes stones roll under their tired feet, but they don't pay attention. All they want is to reach the bottom, find a safe place to pitch their tent and sleep, sleep. Until it's time to get up tomorrow morning and keep on walking all day to get to Chlifa.

"Do we stop here?" Maha asks when they finally reach the bottom of the valley.

"No, I'd go a bit closer to the mountain," replies Karim. "It seems like we're awfully close to the road here. It wouldn't make much sense to have someone spot us when day breaks."

Maha lets out a sigh. Karim's right, of course. But she wants to stop so badly.

She adjusts the shawl around Jad who has slid forward a bit. To do so, she has to let go of Black Beard's rope for a second. Taking advantage of those few seconds, the goat runs off.

"Black Beard! Black Beard! Come back!"

Maha dashes after the goat as it disappears into the night.

Karim, who's still trying to get his bearings, turns impatiently in their direction.

"This is no time to . . . "

A crashing noise drowns out the last part of his sentence. An explosion has rent the night, and its echo reverberates along the valley.

"Maha!" cries Karim. "Maha!"

And he runs like a madman in her direction.

"*El-hamdou li'llah!*" Karim breathes. "Thank God!"

In the beam of his flashlight, Karim has just spotted Maha running in the darkness, her arms stretched out in front of her.

Hearing Karim, she stops and turns to him. Blinded by the light, she closes her eyes. Her small triangular face is streaked with tears.

"It's Black Beard," she says blankly. "I saw her . . . I saw her blow up. We have to get her out of there!"

And she begins running blindly once more.

In one leap, Karim is next to her. Roughly, he grabs her arm.

"You're totally crazy! For all we know, this could be a minefield. You could be blown up just like her. What's the point anyway? She's dead, blown apart, ripped open, in pieces. You can't do a thing for her."

But Maha isn't listening. She's gone wild. Kicking, punching, she fights with ferocious rage. She scratches his face, bites his hand, tries everything to escape his grip.

"Let me go, let me go, let me go!" she screams, verging on hysteria.

And once again her small sharp teeth sink into his hand.

Karim doesn't hesitate any longer. Time to fight fire with fire, he says to himself as he strikes Maha forcefully on the cheek.

Stunned, she sways and stops fighting. Tears well up again in her distraught eyes, and she murmurs, "I have to go after her, I have to find her, I have to bury her. I have to, really I do. We can't leave her there like an animal."

"But she *is* an animal," retorts Karim forcefully. "She is an animal! And I won't let you risk your life, yours and Jad's, for an animal. Do you hear me? Right now you're coming with me. With all this racket, I'm surprised the whole village hasn't shown up on the run. If they do, I don't want to be anywhere near here. I don't know who set the mine, or why, but I'm not sure I want to hang around to find out. Come on."

Maha lets herself be led away without resisting. She shows no enthusiasm, no energy, but at least she keeps moving.

Karim doesn't dare turn the flashlight back on for fear of attracting attention. So they walk blindly along what they assume is the Roman road. Tonight the moon is nowhere to be seen. Karim doesn't know whether to be grateful or sorry.

We can't see a thing, but at least no one can see us either, he says to himself.

After a while, he stops and listens. Not a sound other than night noises, always a bit disquieting. Maybe a far-off murmur, but he can't tell whether it's human voices or the murmuring of a stream.

With the tip of his toe, he tests the ground. He steps off the path, one hand stretched ahead of him, the other still firmly gripping Maha's elbow, and makes his way to a dark mass to his right that can only be a clump of trees.

Under the cover of trees, he risks turning on the flashlight, careful to direct the beam downward. He finds a clearing big enough for the tent, which he puts up hastily. He sets Jad inside and prepares to lead Maha in next when she begins to speak.

The words trickle from her mouth like blood from a wound. Slowly but inexorably.

"She was alive and now she's dead. Tell me, how much time is there between life and death? Between the minute when you're smiling, talking, walking or dreaming and the minute when you're nothing but a carcass, stiff, cold, useless? You know everything. Can you tell me that? She was alive, and then she was dead. I saw her, her shattered head, her broken back, her twisted limbs. In that instant, for the first time, I was filled with love for her. Love and pity, overwhelming pity. And then they turned her over, and I saw her magnificent breasts, untouched. And I was jealous. I was jealous of my sister all over again. I was actually jealous of a corpse, can you imagine that? A corpse?"

Suddenly, she turns to him and starts hammering on his chest with her small, hard fists. And when she starts speaking again, her voice is almost a scream, almost a wail.

"I've always been jealous of Nada for as long as I can remember. She was so beautiful, so sweet, so lovable and smiling. So everything. So much. She reveled in her beauty and sweetness. She found it natural for everyone to follow her with their eyes and flatter her, to love her, to hold her up as an example. And all that time, I was sick with jealousy, sick with spite, sick to death. I wanted to see her disgraced, or humiliated, once, just once. So I could have my chance, too. So that everyone would stop looking at her, her hair, her hips, her madonna's face. To look at me, once, just once. Not just to call me a liar and a thief, but to see the real me. Once, just once."

Maha closes her eyes as though confronted with an unbearable sight.

"And then she was dead. She was broken, soiled, twisted, *and it didn't change a thing.* I was still sick with jealousy. But at the same time, the horror of it all pounds away at my head, my stomach, never, ever stopping. I say to myself, it can't be, it can't be that all that beauty, all that perfection was for nothing. It can't be that her body was for nothing. Just think, the most beautiful girl in the world, and she never knew love. All that beauty wasted, lost. And I'm still here—me, the monster full of jealousy and spite! Don't you find it funny? Don't you find it just horribly funny?"

Maha collapses. Her frail body is shaken with sobs. She keeps repeating that she's a monster, a monster, clawing at the ground with raging fingers.

Karim has stood stock still throughout this explosion of rage and despair, this venting of Maha's vilest, darkest thoughts. He doesn't know what to say. He doesn't know what to do.

Finally, he bends over her small prostrate figure, lightly touches her back, says, "Don't do this to yourself. . . . It's over, all over. You're not a monster, you aren't. You . . . "

Maha straightens up, and her eyes challenge his.

"You're the same. You'd rather it was her and not me making this trip. I dare you to say it isn't so!"

Karim is brought up short.

No, he can't say it isn't so. But with his whole being, he refuses to accept the conclusion Maha has reached.

"This isn't a case of choosing between her and you," he begins with all the conviction he's capable of. "I just wish you were both alive, and that this war had never happened, and that our biggest concern was a physics exam or a poem to write for French class. But that's not the way it is. We've been together for what, two, three days. I chose to come with you, and I don't regret it. Maha, listen to me. You're brave, resourceful, intelligent; you're wonderful with your brother; you're sensitive and funny. I'm not used to girls like you. I have trouble keeping up, but you do me good. You . . . Oh, I don't know, I don't know anymore. But stop doing this to yourself. Stop blaming yourself for everything. You're not a monster full of jealousy and spite, don't you understand? You were jealous of Nada, so what? Everyone's jealous of someone at one time or another. Everyone has dark thoughts one day or another. That's life. It was your bad luck that your sister died when you resented her. But it's not your fault, do you understand me? It just isn't. Stop torturing yourself."

While Karim is speaking, Maha has stopped clawing at the ground with her bare hands, stopped bruising her fingers on the jagged rocks. She stares at Karim with huge, infinitely unhappy eyes in whose depths trembles a tear of incredulous hope.

"They picked her up and took her away. They took them away, Nada, my parents, my aunt Leila, and they threw them into a hole somewhere. I don't even know where. They threw Nada in a hole with her broken body, her untouched breasts, her hair like a black veil. They covered her with earth. They hid her, hid her forever, and I don't even know where. She's rotting somewhere underground, and I'll never see her again, I'll never talk to her again, I'll never be able to tell her I love her. I thought I hated her, but I love her, even if I hate her for dying before I could tell her. Oh, Nada, Nada, Nada . . . "

Karim wraps his arms around the small, trembling body. In class a few years ago, he'd studied *The Little Prince* by Saint-Exupéry. One sentence from that book suddenly comes back to him—"It seemed to me that I was holding a very fragile treasure. It seemed to me, even, that there was nothing more fragile on all the Earth." They aren't just words in a book anymore. They've taken form in the shivering fragile shape of a wounded young girl. Karim rocks her, caresses her, murmurs gentle words, calming words, the words whispered to comfort children.

He feels like crying.

K arim has a wonderful, troubling dream.

He's lying curled up against a woman caressing her breasts. A wonderful sensation of well-being fills him.

Somewhere a baby starts to cry.

Immediately, Karim is on alert.

This isn't a dream; this is reality.

With a shock, Karim realizes he's lying against Maha and that his hand is in fact cupped around a tiny breast. Shame washes over him, but it turns immediately to horror when, against his will, his hand curls in a fleeting caress before tearing itself from the comfort of the warm breast.

He feels like a satyr, a dirty old man taking advantage of a sleeping child.

The best he can hope for is that Maha didn't notice.

Karim casts a rapid glance at Maha's face and jumps when he discovers her solemn gaze on him. . . . If shame could kill, he'd already be dead.

"I . . . I'm sorry," he stammers. "I didn't do it on purpose, I swear. It won't happen again. We . . . we fell asleep on the ground, last night, and . . . "

He doesn't know what else to say. All the explanations in the world wouldn't be enough to excuse the weakness of his body, this shameful betrayal of the trust Maha placed in him.

Still she says nothing, just stares at him with her huge eyes. Her face is smudged with dirt and dried tears, her nails are dirty and chipped, her hands scraped. She's the very image of desolation. And he, Karim, took advantage of her in her sleep!

"Don't look at me that way," he begs. "Please, don't look at me that way. I swear it won't happen again."

Finally, Maha opens her mouth. But the words she utters only trouble Karim more.

"Why did you pull away from me with such horror?" asks Maha in a clear, distinct voice. "Are my breasts that awful? If they'd been Nada's breasts, would you have looked so disgusted?"

Suddenly, Karim has had enough of this jealous, demanding little girl. Enough of her questions and her torment. Enough of her contradictions.

"Your breasts?" he cries in a cruel voice. "What breasts? You don't even have breasts."

Maha reels as though she's been hit. Her face turns cold and hard. Her eyes are frighteningly calm.

"Do you want to know what Nada wrote about the kiss you gave her? 'Not bad, but not as exciting as Rachad's. To tell the truth, Karim is perfect but a bit boring. Too bad, he does have nice eyes.'"

With these words, Maha stands up and goes to get Jad, who is screaming blue murder in the tent.

THEY EAT, TAKE DOWN THE TENT, shoulder their knapsacks. All in an angry silence.

The old Roman road they're following links the villages of Akura and Yammouneh on either side of Mount Lebanon, whose spine they cross via a pass at an altitude of two thousand meters. The road climbs between impressive massifs, among the tallest in the country, their summits almost always covered in snow. To the north is Dahr el-Qadit, and at its base grow the last cedars of Lebanon, age-old symbols of this mountainous country. Behind Dahr el-Qadit is Qornet es-Saouda, the highest point in the country. To the south lies Jebail Sannin, not as high but still majestic.

The climb is gruelling. The silence is soon broken by the sound of their labored breathing, by the occasional scrape of a stone as it rolls under their feet. Resounding in Karim's head are ugly, even cruel words: " . . . less exciting than Rachad's" " . . . not bad, but . . . " " . . . a bit boring." Did Nada really write them, or did Maha make it all up to get back at him? Maha the snoop, the liar. Maha, the unhappy, the desperate. And what does it matter now? Karim notes with sadness that Nada's memory has faded in his mind. The hurt is still there, as well as the regret, but less painful, less sharp.

After a while—two hours, five hours? impossible to say—they reach the pass. Until now, they've done nothing but climb. Now the path descends continuously to Yammouneh, then Chlifa. They've managed to climb to the heart of Mount Lebanon, to the backbone of the country. Strangely enough, Karim feels no sense of triumph. Only immense relief.

They drop their knapsacks, set Jad on the ground at the foot of a huge boulder. Maha brings out the burner, pours water into the small pan.

"I'm going for a walk over there," Karim announces pointing to the mountain rising to their left.

Maha jerks her head up.

"You're abandoning us?"

"I'm not abandoning you. I'm just going for a short walk. I'll be right back down. You don't need to make a big deal out of it."

Maha bites her lip. All of a sudden, she seems lost.

"Come back quickly," she murmurs.

"I'll be back when I get back," replies Karim, annoyed. He sets off.

HE HAS A SUDDEN, DRIVING URGE to climb even higher, stand at the top of the world or, in more modest terms, get a sweeping view of the whole country. It's possible he knows. Some words he'd heard his father say come back to him—" . . . the incredible sense of power you feel seeing the whole country at once, or almost, from the

Mediterranean shore to the Anti-Lebanon foothills."
Karim, too, wants to stand at the top of the world. He,
too, wants to see the sea on one side and the Anti-
Lebanon on the other. He wants to have a first look at
the Beqaa, the huge valley bathed in light that stretches
between the two mountain ranges, Mount Lebanon and
the Anti-Lebanon. He especially wants to keep climbing
to forget the events lower down.

Gradually, he rises above the pass. There are fewer
and fewer trees. Sheets of ice, hollows still covered in
snow appear. Karim climbs slowly, increasingly using
his hands to help himself along. Yesterday's scrapes
come painfully to mind. From time to time, he stands
up and looks around. He can't see Maha and Jad anymore. They're hidden behind the dense foliage at the
foot of the slope. He can't yet see the sea or the Beqaa.
Wherever he looks, he can see nothing but round-
peaked, snow-covered mountains. Now he's on the
snow. He thinks of Maha, whose dream is to make an
angel in the snow. He's not sure this snow is the right
kind. Too hard, too compact. Maha . . .

All through the climb, while he's planting one heel
after another in the snowy crust before taking a cau-
tious step, Karim is reliving the morning's scene. His
troubled awakening, his shame, his angry outburst at
Maha. When really he was angry with himself. The
words he hurled at Maha ring again in his head. "You
don't even have any breasts!" When he'd just discovered
the exact opposite. "You don't even have any breasts!"
When he'd just been aroused by them.

"What of it?" he murmurs, trying now to justify his
words. "After all, I wasn't going to start pawing her just
to make her feel better. Charity has its limits."

But he knows he's being unfair. He knows that between
pawing her "out of charity" and hurling insults at her, he

could have found something, something else to reassure her. But he had only thought of himself.

"I'm scum. I vented on Maha all the horror I felt for myself. I attacked her where she's most vulnerable because I hated myself. What a bastard I am."

He vows to apologize once he's back down. It would be such a shame to end the trip on this vicious note, to erase the moments of friendship and trust. They've come too far, the two of them, to say good-bye as enemies.

Suddenly, Karim can't wait to be back with Maha. He's impatient to talk to her, clear up any misunderstanding. He needs her smile, her forgiveness, her true, open friendship.

He stops again to look around him. Will this climb never end? The higher he goes, the farther he seems to be from the summit. Of course, he's not trying for the summit, just a spot from where he can see the whole region at once, but even this seems to elude him, retreating imperceptibly with every step he takes. How long has he been gone? How long has Maha been waiting for him? Should he push on or turn back?

While he's asking himself these questions, the cry reaches him. A piercing, frightening cry that turns his heart to ice.

"Maha!" he roars in reply.

Only silence answers. A silence still vibrating with the echoes of the terrible cry that shook him.

Now Karim is hurrying downward, but his progress is hindered by the ice, the snow, the steep slopes. He slips, catches himself, slips again and falls, twisting his ankle. He continues, now limping down. "Maha!" he yells every few steps. But still only silence answers.

Finally, he reaches the pass. He wants to run to the boulder where he left Maha and Jad, but suddenly his legs are heavy, terribly heavy. He has trouble lifting his feet, and it has nothing to do with his twisted ankle.

He nears the boulder. Jad is there, lying on his back, waving his legs and arms as he gurgles.

"Maha!" Karim cries out in a hoarse voice. "Maha, where are you? If this is a joke, it isn't funny."

At the same time, he's desperately hoping it is a joke and that Maha will appear from behind a tree crying, "Gotcha!"

"Maha!"

But Maha doesn't appear.

Karim skirts the rock beside the gurgling Jad. His legs are getting heavier by the minute, and his heart is pounding painfully against his chest.

Then he sees her. Immediately, he knows it is not a joke. Not a joke, the half-naked body abandoned behind the rock. Not a joke, the thin trickle of blood along one thigh. Not a joke, the red stream pouring from Maha's slit throat.

Karim falls to his knees in the rocks. He grabs hold of the grass pushing up through the stones. He holds onto the ground to prevent himself from being swallowed by a huge black hole, into the terrifying vortex waiting for him.

The wail torn from his throat awakens every echo in the mountain. A cry of rage, suffering, despair that swells and grows and crashes against the mountain walls, again and again, formidable and powerless.

Neither suffering nor despair stops the world from turning, the birds from singing, the streams from running. Karim keeps on breathing, walking, moving his legs and his arms, doing what the living do.

He covered Maha's nudity. He wrapped a scarf around her mutilated throat. He anchored Jad on his back as best he could. He began to walk, carrying Maha in his arms. He abandoned their knapsacks, useless now. All he kept was the picture of the Tabbara family, the picture of a happy family gathered around a newborn and the postcard of the Lady with the Unicorn. "Wherever you are, I hope there are unicorns, music . . . and goats with black beards," Karim murmured before sliding the postcard into the back pocket of his jeans.

The path is steep down to Yammouneh Lake, now a dried-out lake bed. Karim walks as though in a dream with his double load. He doesn't see where he steps; sometimes he stumbles over jutting rocks. Stones roll under his feet, but he doesn't even notice. He walks, one foot in front of the other, on and on, trying to jostle his precious load as little as possible. His arms go numb. He can't tell anymore whether Maha is heavy or light. Sometimes he feels as though he's carrying a wounded bird, a light, fragile ball of soft, ruffled feathers. But at other times the light-as-air bird grows heavy, and Karim is afraid he'll drop the leaden body dragging at his arms. He flexes his muscles, stiffens his arms, grasps Maha's still-warm body more firmly. He has to keep going. He is almost at the end of the road to Chlifa.

He has no notion of time passing. He knows only that at one point he glimpses a church spire, a mosque's minaret. This is Yammouneh, known to be a proud, fierce village.

Some people—lookouts?—saw him coming and soon

128

one of them approaches him. He's an old man with a heavily seamed face, watchful eyes.

"*Es-salâm aleïkoum*, my son. Peace be with you. You've come from the other side of the mountain?"

"Yes."

"From Akura?"

"From Beirut."

"And where are you going?"

"To Chlifa."

"Chlifa. I see."

Then the old man points to Maha.

"She's dead?"

"Yes."

"What happened?"

"A man, several men maybe. By the pass. I don't know."

"You weren't there."

"No."

"Where were you?"

Karim can't take anymore. Standing still is more exhausting than walking. He sways and would probably have fallen to the ground if the old man hadn't held onto him.

Behind them, some women begin to wail loudly. Karim can't help wondering why. They didn't even know Maha. How dare they grieve her death? Maha's death belongs to him. These women have no right to rob him of it.

"Put her down here," the old man says, pointing to a white cloth at his feet. Karim doesn't know how the cloth got there.

He puts Maha down. Immediately, he feels horribly alone.

He raises his eyes to the old man.

"I was up higher," he finally says in answer to the old man's question. "I wasn't there. She was alone with the baby. I abandoned her."

The old man doesn't respond right away. He looks at the body stretched out at his feet.

"The men who killed her must have been from Akura. Christians. They've been our enemies since the beginning of time."

"Or Syrians," says another man standing off to the side.

"Or outlaws, poachers, thieves," another man suggests. "The mountain has always been a refuge for outlaws."

Why not Israelis? Karim thinks derisively. Or Hezbollah leaders? Or Palestinians? Or the god Mars come down from the heavens for the occasion? Or one of you watching me so closely? What does the killer's identity or nationality matter? She's dead. That's all that matters.

In his heart, he knows who's responsible for her death. Maha didn't die from the knife that slit her throat. She died from abandonment, from words loaded with hatred. He, Karim, was the one who killed her.

"SHE WANTED TO GO TO CHLIFA, she's going to go to Chlifa." This is all Karim would say to the old man's suggestion that they bury Maha there in Yammouneh.

The old man gives in.

While a few women look after Jad, some men go to get the ramshackle cart on which they lay Maha out.

"We could put the baby in here, too," the old man, Ahmed, suggests. But Karim refuses. He'll carry Jad to the end, to Chlifa.

A pitiful convoy sets out for Chlifa, some ten kilometers away. A scrawny donkey pulls the cart. Karim carries Jad. A few men are armed with big rifles.

They follow the uneven paving stones of the road laid between Baalbek and Yammouneh by the Romans a long, long time ago. There at last is the Beqaa Valley spread before Karim, huge and filled with light, but he hardly notices it, no more than he notices the flowers already wilting in the summer heat or the big tortoise watching them pass before hiding in its shell. Karim's eyes are fixed on the cart jolting along a few steps ahead of him, on the white form that was Maha.

The sun has already disappeared on the other side of Mount Lebanon when they reach Chlifa, a miniscule village nestled in the shade at the foot of the mountains.

As soon as the ritual words of welcome are over, Karim asks to see old man Elias.

"Old man Elias?" the man who welcomed them repeats surprised. "What old man Elias?"

"The old man born in this village who returned a few years ago after many years in Beirut. His wife's name is Zahra."

A moment of silence follows Karim's reply.

It feels like the whole village is staring at him wide-eyed with curiosity.

"We are in Chlifa, aren't we?" he finally asks.

"Yes," the man facing him says. "But the man you're looking for, old man Elias, he died six months ago, and his wife joined him a few weeks later. You arrive too late, my son."

"But . . . "

"That woman over there is their niece, Fatima. She'll be able to tell you more than I can."

The man's words whirl around in Karim's mind. *Dead, six months, Fatima.*

If old man Elias and his wife died six months earlier, Maha's parents couldn't have been thinking of sending their children to them. Did Maha make the whole thing up? Had she decided to leave no matter what, without knowing what she'd find when she got here? Or had she just decided to tell him another lie?

Maha's words, spoken on the night they stayed among the moonstones, come back to him: "When I say one thing, I often feel like I could say the opposite and it would be just as true." Lies. Truth. What are they exactly? Words and their opposite. Two sides to reality, one as real as the other? As "true" as the other? "Maha, Maha, you left me with so many questions and so few answers," Karim moans softly before turning toward Elias and Zahra's niece, who takes Jad from his arms and asks him a question he doesn't hear.

THE PREPARATIONS FOR THE BURIAL. After lengthy debate, the elders declare that Maha died *chahîd*, in other words a martyr, and so her body will not be washed before burial. Instead, her body enveloped in a white cloth is placed directly into a hole dug in the ground.

Karim attends the ceremony without really participating. During the reading of the Koran, he talks to Maha in his head. You see, he says to her, for you the rites are being observed. We'll know where you're buried. You're here, in Chlifa, under the shade of a juniper tree. You see, finally, I do know the name of a tree—juniper. It's a beautiful name. And a beautiful tree. More like a big bush with prickly leaves. The type of tree I'd have thought grew in Nordic countries. But, you see, there's one here, and you're buried at its foot. When the wind steals in between its branches, there's a kind of murmuring. It will keep you company when I'm gone. Because I have to go, you see. I . . . See, I have to go, but you, you'll always have the murmur of the wind in the juniper tree. Did I tell you how beautiful the juniper is? You'd love its color. I have to go. There's nothing for me here, you see.

He keeps saying "you see, you see" to one who can no

longer see, trying to explain, to apologize for abandoning her once more.

One of the village men will take them, Jad and him, to the closest Syrian camp. Afterward, Karim hopes to make it to Damascus, the capital of Syria, less than a hundred kilometers away. From there, they'll be able to fly to North America, to Montreal where his parents are.

Fatima, old man Elias's niece, offers to take Jad and look after him as though he were her own son, but Karim refuses.

"No. In a way Maha entrusted him to me. I can't abandon him, too."

"And your parents?" Fatima asks. "What are they going to say when you show up with a baby?"

Karim shrugs his shoulders. His family will just have to accept Jad.

The truth is, he hardly gives it a thought. It's all so far away.

For the time being, all of his thoughts are turned to the moment when he'll have to leave the juniper tree, tear himself away from this plot of earth where Maha will remain forever.

PART III

Life Goes On

Montreal, February – May 1990

I dream of this country where anguish
Is a breath of air
Where to sleep is to plumb the depths
–George Schehadé

KARIM'S DIARY
MONTREAL, SOMETIME IN FEBRUARY 1990

Strange how you lose all notion of time in a hospital bed. Strange, too, how memories flood back. Memories of there and memories of my first months here in Quebec.

The look on my parents' faces when I got off the plane with a baby in my arms! If I'd had the heart to laugh, I would have laughed to see them doing some quick, very quick, mental calculations. Nine months (more or less) plus six or seven months (going by appearances), no, it can't be his son; it's mathematically impossible. They sighed with relief, my father three seconds before my mother. He always was better at mental arithmetic.

Of course they asked questions. I answered without going into details. The Tabbara family died, except for him. I was there. I took him. I brought him. A bit rudimentary maybe, but my parents accepted my explanation. They must really have been relieved to see me safe and sound.

I arrived in Montreal in August. I have no idea what the date was, even if I wasn't in a hospital bed. For the first five or six months, I lived in a total vacuum. In a bubble that isolated me from everything, protected me. I didn't see anything. I didn't hear anything. I didn't do anything. Well, no, I did—I looked after Jad. It was a good thing he was there. Otherwise, I really think I would have gone right out of my mind.

I'd like to be able to say that I thought deeply, questioned the meaning of existence, of life and death. But no. I vegetated. My parents did their best to coax me out of my torpor, get me moving, help me discover the country. I didn't want to see anything. They say autumn's pretty here. Could be. I didn't see a thing.

Finally, after the collective madness of the Christmas holidays, my parents simply forced me to go to the neighborhood high school. Not necessarily to learn anything. Mostly to get me out of my funk. To make me react. Boy, did I react. Beyond their wildest dreams even. So much so that I ended up in this hospital bed. And got caught up against my will in the muddle of "human relations," in the words of our ethics teacher.

There must be a lesson to be learned from all this, but I'm too tired to figure it out now.

FEBRUARY 23

I know what the date is now. I suppose that's a good sign.

Ever since I was transferred to a Montreal hospital—on Valentine's Day as the nurse so kindly pointed out to me—My-Lan has come to see me every day. "My parents are going to think I'm doing an awful lot of studying at Sabine's," she said yesterday with a little laugh.

I'm starting to get used to her different laughs, to her voice, to her almond-shaped eyes. I'm finding it harder to get used to the rest, to what made me hate her in the beginning. Her frail body, her long black hair, certain things she says. So when she comes, I concentrate on her face and her voice. I get her talking.

She's not very talkative, and she's not the kind to go on

and on about her problems or misfortunes. But she did talk about the war in her country, the torture, the dead. She described the odyssey of her trip here. She recalled her first months in Montreal when she couldn't speak a word of French, when everything seemed confusing, often shocking.

First observation: I don't have a monopoly on unhappiness. I hate to have to say it, but I'd almost convinced myself that I was the only person to have seen suffering and death. Imagine that. How full of yourself can you be!

Second observation—in the form of a question: what's the point of wallowing in unhappiness? I realize that for months I draped myself in my unhappiness as if it were a virtue that gave me the right to hold everyone else in contempt. What do I know of the unhappiness of others? By what right did I decide that only my suffering was worthy of interest?

Third observation: whether you live or die, it's your choice. To be or not to be, *as Mr. Shakespeare said. I have no idea what he had in mind when he wrote those words, but they seem to fit what I'm discovering. When I woke up in that hospital in the Laurentians, I was almost sorry I wasn't dead. Now I look back on that almost as a form of cowardice. I don't like that word. Who decides what is or isn't cowardice? Or what courage is? Or what to admire? You were right, Maha. Sometimes now, I, too, feel like I could say the opposite of what I'm saying, and it would be just as true. It tends to complicate things a bit but doesn't make them any less interesting. Actually, it even tends to make them more interesting. Where was I? Living or dying. In fact, for six months I was more like the living dead. I couldn't make up my mind. I tried to live cut off from others, memories, night-mares and remorse, cut off from life. It couldn't last.*

I still don't know why we're alive. Maybe I'll never know. But it seems to me we don't have the right to let ourselves die. If only out of respect for all those who die but wanted to live. For now, that's reason enough for me. I choose to live because Maha and Nada are dead. And their parents, their Aunt Leila and all the others I don't know. I choose to live so their deaths haven't been in vain, so they won't be forgotten. I choose to live to tell their lives to Jad, who's just taken his first steps, and there's nothing more incredible than a baby's first steps. Oh, Maha, Maha, you didn't even see Jad take his first step!

FEBRUARY 28

Back home again. I'm still not in great shape. I feel like an old man suffering from rheumatism and cachexia. I don't really know what cachexia means, but it's a great word. Maha would have loved it. I realize that I often store up words, sounds and images for her.

With my return home, My-Lan's visits came to an end. I miss her visits more than I imagined. I need My-Lan. She's my link to the world. She let me build a bridge between there and here. No small feat.

But it's not the end of the world either, as they say here. In other words, I'm not in love with her as the nurses (indulgently) seem to think. My parents, too (relieved—he isn't dead, he's getting back to normal—but worried—a Lebanese boy and an Asian girl, how's that going to work?). Even Béchir, to whom I sent a brief report on the past few weeks and on my feats on North American soil.

"Well, old buddy," Béchir wrote in reply, "you're certainly not dying of boredom deep in your forests! Does this mean that I'll soon be receiving the list of twenty-one things you like over there and that the list will begin with 'My-Lan'? So what's your girlfriend like? Since I've already told you all about Lolote, I expect you to do the same. Glibly yours, etc., etc., etc."

Lolote! At first I thought he was joking, but I have to face facts—my friend Béchir is in love with a girl whose name is Lolote. It's hard to swallow, but, hey, I'll manage. That's the mark of a true friend.

Enough fooling around. No, I'm not in love with My-Lan, although that doesn't stop me from caring a great deal for her and waiting impatiently to see her again. That's all.

L ife goes on. Almost like before. But that "almost" makes a world of difference.

Obviously, the earth wouldn't stop turning just because a fight broke out and one guy almost killed another.

There were legal and administrative hassles. I suppose it was inevitable. I don't know the details. I'm not interested. But everything seems to have gotten back to normal quickly. Some people say Karim's family didn't press charges, and the whole affair was classified as an "accident." Other people claim that Dave has to report to a judge (or a police officer, or a psychologist, or a social worker depending on who's telling the story) every two (five, ten, thirty, fifty—need I say more) weeks. The truth is that no one knows all the ins and outs of the matter.

So I will, as usual, stick to the most reliable accounts.

We made the trip back from the class ski outing in total shock. A fight, a knifing, a serious casualty. We had trouble absorbing it all, realizing it had really happened in our class between guys we knew or thought we knew. If I weren't leery of making pronouncements, I'd say that Violence Just Erupted In Our Lives. A great big title in red and black letters.

In the following days, everyone treated us like convalescents, gingerly, with kid gloves. No exams, no reprimands, no overly long assignments. It was as if they were afraid of seeing the rest of us explode one after the other.

Dave came back to class first. Not as in-your-face as usual. Not totally subdued, of course (you can't expect miracles) but not as much of a pain as before. Maybe the story about the judge, lawyer or whoever is true. Or maybe he just had the scare of his life.

Karim didn't come back till March. Strangely enough, he's both more visible and less talked about than before. He's more present; he participates in activities and discussions more. I wouldn't go so far as to say he's the livewire of the class, but he joins in the group. He even seems to be striking up a friendship with Simon, one of the nice guys in our class. On the other hand, he's lost his desert prince look. Kind of a shame, but I suppose you can't have both a terribly romantic figure and a guy who finally acts human in the same person. The upshot is, after the rather morbid curiosity of the first few days, everyone quit watching his every move and expression, and started to treat him normally. Even Nancy gave up trying to seduce him. She jumped up to hug him as soon as he got back and planted a long kiss on the "hero's" lips—as she called him—but Karim didn't respond to her attack with much enthusiasm. She decided he must be gay. What I like about Nancy is the wonderful simplicity of her reasoning. It sure must make life easier for her.

Others, however, are convinced Karim has a soft spot for My-Lan. First because he came to her rescue. Then because he spends a lot of time with her. To me, that seems to be an overly simplistic line of reasoning, too, but basically, what do I know. I'm better off keeping my opinions to myself.

One last detail. Karim and Dave are civil to each other. They aren't the best of pals, which would be pretty surprising after all, but they don't come out swinging every time they see each other. They even play soccer together!

If I had to sum up the atmosphere in the class or the changes over the year, I'd say we seem to breathe a bit easier. It's definitely not heaven on earth, but it isn't the cold, artificial place we all lived in without ever touching or knowing anything about each other. We talk more. We get more involved. In French, we're putting on a play called "I ain't racist, but . . . " It won't change the world. It just might help us understand the world we live in a bit better. The people we live with, too. At least it's a lot better than fighting each other.

KARIM'S DIARY
MONTREAL, A FARAWAY LAND
MAY 15, 1990

You're a pain, Béchir, old friend, and that's the truth.

But patience has its rewards. Is that really a proverb? If not, I claim authorship.

Twenty-one things you asked for. Well, here they are (in no particular order):

1   *spring (because of winter, which I loathe, detest, execrate, etc.)*
2   *Mount Royal*
3   *sugar pie*
4   *the laughter of certain girls (not all!)*
5   *peace*
6   *a guy called Simon who's becoming a good friend (don't worry, he hasn't taken your place completely . . . although he's much less of a pain than you are)*
7   *soccer (that's what they call football here)*
8   *swimming pools*
9   *certain girls' legs (not all!)*
10 *Saturday mornings in bed with a book*
11 *Rue Sainte-Catherine and the buildings downtown*
12 *movie theaters*
13 *biology class (by the way, in your last letter, besides reaming me out for not having sent you my list of twenty-one things that I like here yet, you reminded me that you still intend to get your engineering degree and go back to Lebanon to rebuild our battered country; keep me posted about your plans; we can meet there in a few years when you're an engineer and I'm a doctor; I've been thinking about it a*

lot for a while, and I think I'd really like patching up battered bodies, souls, too, maybe; anyhow, we'll see)

14 *Rue Saint-Laurent*

15 *snowstorms (and don't try to tell me I'm contradicting myself)*

16 *bike paths*

17 *the freedom to come and go, to get involved or not*

18 *peace (yes and yes and yes)*

19 *certain girls' hair (not all!)*

20 *the peaceful sound of cars at night*

21 *(censored)*

Satisfied now?

I do insist on pointing out, however, that I hate and will always hate hockey, peanut butter, soap operas and English class.

–Karim